"If I kiss you again, ... stop there."

"Promises, promises," she murmured.

There was a sense of danger here that he didn't encounter on the street. On the street, he knew the odds, knew the chances he was taking. "I'm not kidding, Kelsey."

She could feel her heart beginning to race. Her voice was husky with anticipation as she said, "I certainly hope not."

Kelsey's lips were only inches from his. So close he could all but taste them against his own.

His body throbbed. How long could he resist something he wanted so badly?

"Whatever happens here is on your head."

"I accept full responsibility," she whispered. As she spoke, her lips lightly grazed his.

Dear Reader,

I didn't want to write this book. As long as I didn't tell Kelsey's story, I had one more book in the Marlowes' saga. But it wasn't fair to Kelsey so, here we are, watching the last of Kate Marlowe's children find her soul mate.

Kelsey Marlowe has a tough time finding love. She's feisty, independent and has four brothers eager to interrogate and dismiss every suitor. But now the Marlowe boys are all married, and Kelsey has become her own worst enemy in the pursuit of love. When she does find an irresistible man, she discovers that he comes with not just baggage, but scars. Despite the chemistry, the romance seems doomed before it ever takes off. Only Kate can see through the smoke screens between her daughter and the fine young police officer. How can a mother help bring them together?

I hope you enjoy this last installment of KATE'S BOYS... and daughter, too. As ever, I thank you for reading and wish you someone to love who loves you back.

All the best,

Marie Ferrarella

MARIE FERRARELLA

A LAWMAN FOR CHRISTMAS

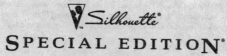

SPECIAL EDITION®

Published by Silhouette Books

America's Publisher of Contemporary Romance

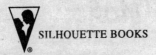

SILHOUETTE BOOKS

ISBN-13: 978-0-373-65488-8

Recycling programs
for this product may
not exist in your area.

A LAWMAN FOR CHRISTMAS

Visit Silhouette Books at www.eHarlequin.com

Printed in U.S.A.

Selected books by Marie Ferrarella

MARIE FERRARELLA

This *USA TODAY* bestselling and RITA® Award-winning author has written more than 200 novels for Silhouette Books, some under the name Marie Nicole. Her romances are beloved by fans worldwide. Visit her Web site at www.marieferrarella.com.

To
Pat Teal
with thanks
for opening the door.
Here's to another
twenty-eight years.

Chapter One

Omigod, omigod, omigod.

The single word repeated through her brain like an old-fashioned vinyl record spinning on a record player, its needle stuck in a groove.

"Calm down, Kelsey. It's going to be fine. It's all going to be fine."

The latter words Kelsey Marlowe said out loud, as if hearing the reassuring echo about the car while she tore out of the school parking lot would somehow help her gather herself together.

It didn't.

She was having trouble focusing, both on the road and on the thoughts firing through her brain like pellets from a shotgun.

Her mother's phone call a few minutes ago had really rattled her.

Kelsey had been more than halfway down the hall on her way to the exit before she remembered that she had to get someone to cover her class for her. She'd left twenty-eight highly charged eight- and nine-year-olds in the hands of the school secretary. She'd had to come running back, wasting precious minutes, to make the request.

Clutching the steering wheel, she roared down the freeway.

C'mon, Kelse, get a grip!

In all her twenty-six years, she couldn't remember *ever* being this scared, this nervous. Especially because her mother had begged her not to call any of her brothers and definitely not her father. Kate Marlowe didn't want any of them knowing that she was in the E.R. at Blair Memorial.

Her soft-spoken mother was her rock. Rocks didn't get sick. They didn't call from a hospital emergency room. Rocks were supposed to be just that: rocks, meant to go on forever until the end of time.

Dragging her hand through her wayward blond hair, Kelsey took in another deep breath, this time holding it to the count of fifteen before she released it. It didn't help.

Despite Kelsey's urgings, her mother told her that she didn't want to go into any kind of detail over the telephone. Instead, she just repeated her initial request for her to come to the hospital as quickly as possible.

That in and of itself made her extremely nervous. Her mother *never* asked for help. Petite, blonde and as quietly stubborn as all her Irish forbearers put together,

Kate Llewellyn Marlowe believed in always handling her own emergencies. Not only that, but she insisted on taking on any and all emergencies that any family member or friend was going through.

As far back as Kelsey could remember, her mother had always been a dynamo who absolutely nothing, no matter how large, could rattle, sidetrack or damage. The woman had put multitasking on the map, doing it long before it ever had a label affixed to it.

Something was really, really wrong.

"I'm going to stay calm. I'm going to stay calm," Kelsey said over and over again under her breath as if it were some sort of soothing mantra.

Glancing at the speedometer, Kelsey realized that she was going fifteen miles over the speed limit. Instead of slowing down, she looked in her rearview mirror, searching for police. As far as she could see, not a single police car or motorcycle was in sight.

Thank God for small favors, she thought.

"Now if you only grant me one big one, I promise never to ask You for anything else again. Ever," she underscored. "And this time, I'll make it stick," Kelsey swore, remembering the short-lived duration of her last deal with God.

This was different.

She'd been younger then. And besides, ultimately, what she'd prayed for—begged for—hadn't been granted. Back then, the so-called "favor" she'd begged God for involved the man, a policeman, she'd fallen in love with. A man who hadn't made her his wife the way he'd promised because he already had one of those. He'd just failed to mention that little fact to her.

Why was she thinking about that now?

"C'mon, Kelse, slow down and *focus*." A minute later, she realized Blair Memorial was only two miles away now. Her heart continued hammering as she drove.

Getting there seemed to take forever.

When she finally reached the hospital, Kelsey made a right turn onto the street and went straight to the six-story parking structure. Once parked, Kelsey hurried out of the parking structure. She wove her way through the compound, impatiently darting around several slow-moving vehicles. Finally reaching the emergency-room entrance, she blew out a long breath. She still couldn't calm down.

The electronic doors sprang open the instant she approached them. Kelsey searched the immediate area for someone official who could point her in the direction of the emergency area.

She settled on an older, white-haired woman in a pink smock sitting behind a desk. Short, plump, pleasant and round-faced, at first glance the woman could have easily doubled as Cinderella's fairy godmother.

"You have my mother here." Kelsey quickly realized that the statement had come out like an accusation. Nerves again, she thought. "I mean, my mother called me to say she was in the emergency room here." Words were colliding on her tongue. Was she even making any sense? "Please, I need to see her. She's in the emergency room," Kelsey prodded, surprised she wasn't shouting. "My guess is that she's still there. Otherwise, she would have called me again to say she was leaving. Her name is Kate Marlowe," Kelsey said.

The slightly perplexed look on the older woman's face dissolved into a smile. "And you'd be right. There she is, right there." The woman tapped the screen triumphantly. "She's in the emergency room all right." Turning from her desk, the woman pointed to the left. "You need to speak to that young lady sitting over there. She'll be able to help you."

Kelsey managed a "Thank you" before making her way over to the woman indicated.

"Maybe you can help me," Kelsey began. The nurse didn't look up from the keyboard. Her fingers flew across the keys. Kelsey suppressed the urge to grab the nurse's hands and still them. "My mother called me from your emergency room—"

Only the nurse's perfectly shaped eyebrows rose in a silent query. Her eyes remained on the screen as she continued typing.

"Name?"

"Kate Marlowe. My mother's name is Kate Marlowe," Kelsey elaborated, in case the nurse thought she was giving her own name.

"Marlowe," the nurse murmured under her breath, typing. "She's still here in the E.R.," the nurse confirmed. "Bed number fifteen." For the first time, the woman looked up. Kelsey noted that the nurse had kind eyes. "If you want to see her, I'll buzz you in," she offered.

"Bless you," Kelsey exhaled.

The nurse flashed her an understanding smile. The moment the buzzer sounded, Kelsey raced through the door.

Once inside the E.R., she stopped dead. There was a sea of beds in front of her. They ran along on both sides of the wall. Some were hidden behind white curtains that hung from the ceiling, and others were out in the open—and, for the most part, empty.

"Can I help you?" an orderly asked, coming up on Kelsey's right.

"I'm looking for bed number fifteen," she told him. "Which way would I go?"

He pointed to the rear of the wing. "Bed number fifteen's on the left. In the back," he added.

"Thank you." Kelsey was off and moving before the orderly finished speaking.

Please let her be all right, please let her be all right, she silently repeated, making a beeline for the bed the orderly had pointed out.

As she approached, Kelsey thought she saw someone standing by the bed. The next second she realized that it was a uniformed policeman.

The bed couldn't belong to her mother, she thought. There was no reason for a policeman to be talking to her mother.

Was there?

It *was* her mother's bed. Kelsey recognized the form before she had a clear view of the woman's face. Her mother had a way of tilting her head when she was listening to someone talk. It had always created a feeling of comfort and well-being for her, Kelsey thought.

Only her mother, lying flat on her back in a hospital emergency room, would be trying to be comfort another person.

Her stomach tied itself into a tight knot.

Keeping her eyes on bed number fifteen, Kelsey made her way around several of the hospital staff. She felt her shoulders stiffen and tension coursed through her body the way it always did whenever she saw a policeman these days.

Who was this man?

From the expression on her mother's face, it appeared that she knew the officer. Knew him and liked him. But then again, she'd never known her mother to meet anyone she didn't like. Kate Marlowe always looked for the good in a person and she had a huge heart.

But that still didn't answer her question, Kelsey thought.

What was a policeman doing here, talking to her mother? Granted, Kate Marlowe had always had the kind of face that drew words out of virtual strangers, but it would have been a far more likely scenario if her mother were on the receiving end of an orderly's life history. Or if one of the nurses was standing there, baring her soul to her mother. Not a policeman.

Oh God, was this worse than she thought?

Chapter Two

The next moment, Kelsey felt the kind of surge that coursed through the veins of a lioness when she perceived that one of her cubs was being threatened. Kelsey might have been the youngest in the family, but she had always been fiercely protective, even though not a single one of her four brothers or her parents ever needed protecting.

Until now.

"Excuse me," she said, addressing the back of the police officer's head. "Is there a problem here?"

Whatever answer Officer Morgan Donnelly had at the ready vanished the moment he glimpsed the woman who belonged to the angry voice. His smile was slow, appreciative as he looked her over from head to toe. It occurred to him that she resembled the woman he was talking to. A kid sister perhaps?

"No, no problem at all," he told her.

Giving the sandy-haired patrolman with the X-ray eyes and unreadable expression a cold glare, Kelsey drew herself up to her full, rather unimposing five-foot-four height. The next second, she was Kate's shaken daughter, trying to hide just how upset she really was.

"Mom," she cried, "you scared me half to death." There didn't seem to be any bruises that she could see. Why was her mother here? And what did it have to do with the cop with the X-ray eyes? "Are you all right?"

"I am now," Kate told her, "thanks to Officer Donnelly." Smiling, her mother nodded at the young policeman.

"Oh."

Well, that snuffed out a good deal of Kelsey's animosity toward the officer. Because of her experience with Dan, her view of policemen in general was tainted. She'd just assumed that the young officer at her mother's bedside was somehow responsible. Maybe he'd cut her mother off and caused her to have an accident.

Still, her mother was grateful to him. Drawing herself up again, Kelsey nodded at him. "Thank you," she said stiffly.

Reaching up, Kate wove her fingers through her daughter's and squeezed her hand. "Honey, I didn't want to call and upset you, but the doctor said I had to call someone to take me home and I just couldn't call your father or your brothers."

"I offered to take your mother home," the officer

said, his voice solemn but kind as he nodded at Kate, "but she refused."

"I couldn't impose on you any further," Kate protested. "You've already done enough for me."

Just what did her mother mean by "enough"? Kelsey bit back the urge to ask her. "Not that I mind being the one you turn to, Mom, but why couldn't you call any of them?"

Kate didn't answer immediately. Instead, she raised her eyes to her daughter's face. "If I told you it's because they're all busy working, would you believe me?"

This was a tough one, Kelsey thought. Her gut told her something was going on. "Well, I've never known you to lie about anything, so I guess I'd have to." She paused, studying her mother. Kate Marlowe looked tired and worn. Tired she'd seen before, but in her experience, her mother had *never* looked worn. Something was wrong. "But you are lying, aren't you?"

To Kelsey's surprise, a hint of embarrassment colored her mother's cheeks. Another first. One that made her uneasy.

"I didn't want to upset them," her mother told her.

"But you're okay with upsetting me?"

Still dazed by what the doctor had told her, Kate chose her words carefully. "No, but I know I can count on you. You're a woman, too."

Kelsey stared at her, stunned. She'd fought most of her life to be thought of as anything other than "a little girl" or "the baby of the family." She would have taken pride in the breakthrough moment if it wasn't for the nagging feeling that something was really wrong.

Kelsey glanced toward the patrolman standing at the foot of her mother's hospital bed. Why was he still here? Had he given out his quota of tickets for the day and now had nothing to do? It was on the tip of her tongue to ask him. She had never fully mastered tact. That was her mother's domain.

For her mother's sake, she did her best to sound polite. She succeeded. Moderately. "Just how do you figure into all this?"

"Kelsey." Dismayed, Kate chided her only daughter with the tone of her voice.

The officer raised a hand in her mother's direction, indicating that he didn't mind being questioned. "That's okay, Kate."

"Kate?" Kelsey echoed, her mercurial temper flaring. She hated figures of authority who patronized those they felt were beneath their station. "That's Mrs. Marlowe to you."

"Kelsey." This time the reprimand was a little more obvious. Her tone was sharper. "I'm sorry, Morgan. My daughter tends to be a little hotheaded."

"Daughter," Morgan repeated, impressed. "When she first came in, I thought she was your kid sister."

Kelsey rolled her eyes. Just what did this cop hope to gain by flattering her mother? Granted the woman had a youthful aura about her, she always had, and she really didn't look near her age, but that didn't change the fact that she thought the man was up to no good. She felt it in her bones. Whatever it was, he wasn't going to get away with it. Not while she was around.

"Thank you for the compliment," Kate said, "but I still want to apologize for her." Again she linked her fingers with her daughter's. "She doesn't mean to sound rude. She's just upset."

Morgan dismissed the need for an apology. "That's all right. I run up against that all the time." He turned to look at Kelsey. "Just not usually from someone as pretty as your daughter."

Kelsey heard a little bit of a twang in his voice. A transplant, Kelsey thought with the pinch of snobbery reserved for those who were California natives.

"Flattery's not going to get you anywhere," Kelsey informed him flatly. Her hands were on her hips as she turned toward him. "Now, once and for all, why are you here?"

His eyes shifted over to Kate. The mother was far less combative than her daughter. "I'm just making sure your mother's all right, that's all."

Kelsey turned to look at her mother. "Then something *did* happen." Kelsey ignored the policeman's presence as she took both her mother's hands in hers. Her mother's fingers felt cold. "Mom, what's going on? Talk to me," she pleaded. "What happened and why is he hovering over you like some tarnished guardian angel?" Her eyes narrowed, hoping to get at the truth quickly. "Were you in an accident?"

Kate reached up to cup her daughter's cheek. "Almost," she confessed. "But I'm all right now."

Kelsey glared at the officer expectantly. He didn't disappoint her.

"Your mother ran into a hedge right off University Drive."

Her mother was an excellent driver. She, not her father, had taught all five of them how to drive. This didn't make any sense. "On purpose?"

Kate searched for a way to explain without upsetting Kelsey any further. But there just wasn't any other way. "I fainted."

Fear rose up like a huge black shadow, blotting out everything else. It gripped her heart. Her imagination instantly envisioned all sorts of awful scenarios.

"Mom!"

Her eyes quickly swept over her mother, searching for telltale signs of the injuries her mother must have sustained. But except for her unnaturally pale color, Kate Marlowe looked as lovely as ever. Just shaken.

"It's all over, honey," Kate soothed. "Officer Donnelly was kind enough to come to my rescue. He insisted on bringing me to the hospital instead of making me wait for the paramedics to arrive."

The last remnants of Kelsey's anger and protectiveness faded. Instead, she felt vulnerable and unarmed. To make matters worse, she knew that she needed to apologize.

"Thank you," she said as warmly as she could manage. "I'm sorry I jumped to conclusions. It's just when I saw you looming over my mother—I mean, standing over her like that—I just—"

Morgan waved away her halting apology. Kate's

daughter appeared far too uncomfortable. "No need to apologize. If it makes you feel any better, I *was* following her to give her a ticket. When I noticed her ahead, she was weaving erratically on the road. My first thought was that she was driving under the influence."

Kelsey's temper was back, flaring before she could rein it in. "At ten o'clock in the morning?"

"Oh, you'd be surprised," he told her. "It's always five o'clock somewhere."

Kelsey didn't bother acknowledging his statement. Instead, she asked her mother, "You're not taking any new medication, are you?" Kelsey had moved out of the house three months ago and had been busy setting up her new life. That meant she was no longer privy to her parents' day-to-day lives. She felt a sudden pang at that. Maybe if she were still living at home—

Kate laughed softly. "Now you sound like the attending physician." She went over the same thing she'd said to the E.R. doctor. "No, no meds, no fever, no explanation. I only fainted once in my life and that was when I was first pregnant with you."

"Well, then—"

Kelsey stopped abruptly, her mind brought to a skidding halt by the thought. Her mother wasn't— No, she couldn't be.

The next moment, she banished the very idea as being far too ridiculous to voice out loud. "Maybe it was something you ate."

Kate pressed her lips together, nodding. "Maybe." There was no conviction in her voice.

Kelsey took a deep breath. "So, can I spring you now?" The sooner she got her mother out of here, the better they would both feel.

Kate was anxious to leave herself. She looked out toward the aisle. "Just as soon as the doctor discharges me."

Kelsey glanced around, but the only hospital personnel she saw in the general vicinity were nurses. "And what's the doctor waiting for?"

"He said he wanted to examine the results of a few lab tests and the X-ray he had me take," Kate said.

Was it her imagination, or did her mother sound evasive? Kelsey thought.

Across from her, the stony-faced policeman seemed to come to life. "Well, there's no point in my hanging around any longer. I'm still on duty," Morgan told Kate. "Be careful out there, Mrs. Marlowe," he said politely. Casting a side glance at Kelsey, he looked down at her left hand before adding, "You, too, Ms. Marlowe."

Turning on his heel, Morgan was about to leave when the E.R. physician on call, Dr. Samuel David, came to join them. Seeing the doctor, Morgan decided to linger a moment longer. Closure was something he was ever striving for.

Dr. David smiled at his patient. If he was remotely curious as to the identity of the woman beside her, he didn't show it. "Mrs. Marlowe, I've just confirmed our suspicions."

"Suspicions?" Kelsey echoed.

"About why she fainted." As if suddenly becoming

aware of her, the doctor paused, looking from the woman in the bed to the one standing beside her. "My God, you look just like her."

"I take that as a compliment," both Kate and Kelsey said together then laughed. For just the briefest of moments, the tension they both felt eased.

"And well you should," Dr. David agreed, his tone not sure which of them he was speaking to. And then he cleared his throat. "Well, back to the diagnosis—"

Kelsey felt her heartbeat quickening. *Oh God, please don't make it anything bad.* Out loud, she whispered, "Is it serious?" as she looked at the doctor.

"Depends on how you view this kind of thing," Dr. David said. "Personally, I think it's very serious."

Kelsey reached for her mother's hand again. She willed her mother her strength, but in reality Kate Marlowe was always the strong one. Her mother was the foundation of her family.

She held her breath, waiting to hear the doctor tell them something that could quite possibly change their lives forever.

"Bringing a child into the world is a very serious business," Dr. David continued, his black eyes sweeping from mother to daughter and then back again.

"A child?" Kelsey cried, stunned, confused. "What child? Where?"

Without realizing it, she tightened her grasp on her mother's hand, squeezing it so tight that her own fingers began to ache.

"Your mother's child," the E.R. physician said, and

then he chuckled. "And I would think the 'where' is self-explanatory."

Feeling as if the floor had just melted away beneath her feet, Kelsey stared at her mother. "You're pregnant?" she cried. Before her mother could say anything, Kelsey shifted her eyes to the doctor. "She's pregnant?" she cried incredulously.

Dr. David smiled kindly and nodded. "It would seem so."

Kelsey felt as if she'd just leaned against the mirror and fallen through the looking glass. "But that's not possible."

"Why not?" the policeman asked.

Kelsey didn't know what stunned her more: the fact that her mother was pregnant at fifty or that the muscle-bound cop with the X-ray vision had the audacity to question her reaction.

Her eyes flashed as she said, "Because—because she's my mother and she's already got five kids and this part of her life was supposed to be over." Pushing past the policeman, she rounded the foot of the bed to get closer to the doctor. "Doctor, I don't mean to doubt you, but are you sure there's been no mistake? Lab results get switched all the time. Maybe you got my mother's tests mixed up with someone else's."

"Granted there are mix-ups on occasion," the doctor allowed, "but I'm happy to say, we have a low incidence of that. Blair Memorial has been ranked one of the leading hospitals in the country for the last ten years in a row now." He turned to face Kate. "You are pregnant, Mrs. Marlowe," he said with finality. "You'll need to start right away with pre-natal care. I could give you the name of an excellent doctor—"

"I already have one," Kate replied, her words coming out slowly, impeded by the half dozen scattered thoughts racing through her mind. Taking a deep breath didn't help steady her nerves. She looked at Kelsey. "Your father's going to be stunned."

"He's not the only one," Kelsey replied. Try as she might, she couldn't visualize her mother "in the family way." There were photographs in the family albums of her being pregnant, but that was a long time ago. And, at the time, her mother had been younger than she was.

Breaking the tension, Morgan leaned forward and took Kate's hand in his. "Congratulations, Mrs. Marlowe. A baby is a wonderful thing," he told her with feeling.

Kelsey laughed shortly. "Spoken like a man who's never had one." Where did he get off, anyway, voicing an opinion? He was a stranger.

To Kelsey surprise, Morgan looked as if he was about to say something in response, then obviously changed his mind. Instead, he merely nodded at Kate. "Good luck to you," he said as he began to withdraw.

Sensing that the E.R. physician wanted to go over a few more things with her mother before she was signed out, Kelsey stepped to the side.

The policeman had turned around to leave. Kelsey suddenly remembered something.

"Wait," she called after the departing policeman, then hurried to catch up to him. "Officer Donnelly, was it?"

Morgan stopped and turned around. "Morgan," he corrected. He liked things to be professional and formal, but in her case, something prompted him to be more familiar.

"Morgan," Kelsey repeated, inclining her head. "Where's my mother's car now? You didn't have it towed away, did you?" If it had been towed away, there would be a mountain of paperwork and red tape before she could get the car back, not to mention that there would be a hefty fine.

"No, it's still where she left it. Just a little past the intersection of University Drive and Campus Road." Morgan paused, debating.

It had been a slow morning. No reason to believe the afternoon wasn't going to be the same. Bedford was deemed one of the safest cities in the country. Helping out a citizen came under the heading of good public relations. The chief was always after them to work with the citizens and promote goodwill.

"I could take you over there if you like," he volunteered, "and then you could drive it to your mother's house."

"Then what would I do with the car I drove here?"

"Right." Morgan had forgotten about that. He thought for a moment. The solution was simple. "Tell you what, you bring your mother home first, and I'll follow you in the squad car. After you get her settled, I'll take you to your mother's car."

That was really going out of his way, she thought. Once upon a time, she would have taken his offer at face value. But that was before Dan. "And why would you do that?" she asked suspiciously.

"The Bedford police department aims to please," he told her simply. And then he looked at her for a long moment. She felt as if he were peering right into her. "Are you always this suspicious?"

"Only when things seem to be out of sync." And then she considered her mother. Talk about out of sync. "A baby," she murmured, shaking her head.

He was still scrutinizing her, still looking into her soul. Kelsey bristled at the thought.

"Why does that bother you so much?" he asked, and then guessed at the reason. "You're the youngest, aren't you?"

Kelsey squared her shoulders. "That has nothing to do with it."

In his opinion, that had a great deal to do with it. But he had no desire to get into any sort of a discussion with her about it. He had a feeling she did not give up easily. "If you say so."

Kelsey caught her lower lip between her teeth. "It's just that…"

Morgan anticipated her words. "Don't say she's too old," he cautioned. "Your mother looks like a young, vital woman."

That was only half the picture. "Who already has a life and five children."

"Now she'll have six."

Kelsey stared up at Morgan. He certainly didn't sound like a typical male his age. She placed him in his late twenties. Most men in that age bracket fiercely resisted anything that seemed remotely close to domestication.

"You like babies?" she asked, studying him as she waited for an answer.

She had a long wait ahead of her. Rather than answer, he nodded toward her mother's bed. "The E.R. doctor's leaving. Better help your mother get ready. I'll wait for you at the E.R.'s registration desk." He pointed toward doors that led outside the emergency room.

Without waiting for a response, Morgan walked away, heading toward the doors. Leaving her with a basketful of questions.

Chapter Three

"He seems like a very nice man," Kate commented to Kelsey.

Morgan had helped Kate out of the wheelchair that the hospital's insurance policy required for all inpatients leaving the premises, then gently eased her into her daughter's car. True to his word, the young policeman followed behind them as Kelsey drove her home.

Kelsey lifted one shoulder in a dismissive half shrug. "He's okay for a policeman."

She glanced up into her rearview mirror. If she was hoping that he'd taken off instead of following them, she was disappointed. In true law enforcement style, Donnelly drove a sensible distance behind them.

Kelsey sped up.

So did he.

She had a gut feeling that Officer Morgan Donnelly was not an easy man to shake.

She couldn't really put into words why, but the fact that he trailed behind them annoyed her. Kelsey knew she was unreasonable, that the policeman had been extremely accommodating and made things easy for her. She should be grateful.

But policemen as a species were not really high on her approval list right now. Not since she'd broken up with Dan. Moreover, she wasn't exactly in the best of moods. For one thing, she was still shaken up by having to rush to the hospital, not knowing what to expect when she got there. For another, the news of her mother's current delicate condition had completely thrown her for a loop.

If one of her brothers had told her that they were expecting, she would have been instantly overjoyed. This was something else again. It would take getting used to.

Kelsey could feel her mother's gaze.

Glancing briefly to her right, Kelsey asked, "What?"

"Since when do you have something against policemen?" Kate asked.

Ordinarily, her life was an open book. She and her mother were more than family—they were friends and she valued her mother's insight and judgment. But this had been a very personal hurt. Because she hadn't wanted to endure her brothers' teasing, not to mention their questions, no one had even known she was seeing Dan at the time. And afterward, when she'd felt like an idiot because Dan had been stringing her along, well, she didn't feel like sharing that, either.

It definitely wasn't a topic she wanted to raise now.

Kelsey shook her head. "Mom, I don't want to waste time talking about policemen."

Kate smiled. "What do you want to waste time talking about?"

"I don't want to waste time at all—" Kelsey realized that her voice was tense. But then, this wasn't an everyday situation. Stopping at a stoplight at an intersection, she slanted another look at her mother. "Mom, what are you going to do?"

Clearly puzzled by the question, Kate asked, "About?"

"World peace," Kelsey retorted, her tension getting the best of her. And then she flushed. "Sorry. Didn't mean to be so flip. About the baby, Mom. What are you going to do about the baby?"

Her mother never hesitated. "Start eating healthier, exercising more. And giving up that glass of wine I always have with your father at dinner." The light turned green and Kelsey pressed down on the gas pedal. There was just the slightest shift in her mother's voice as she asked, "What else would I do?"

How in heaven's name do you ask your mother if she was considering an alternative to giving birth? For one of the few times in her life, Kelsey felt tongue-tied. Taking a breath, she forced herself to forge ahead.

The words came out haltingly. "Well, I thought maybe, because you're not twenty-four anymore…"

Reading between the lines, Kate took pity on her. "I

know how old I am, Kelsey. And the doctor says I'm definitely healthy enough to go the distance."

Yes, her mother was healthy and energetic and all those good things. But having a baby was a life-altering decision. Her mother had to know that. "What about after the distance? This doesn't just end with delivery."

Kate made no attempt to hide her amusement. "Are you under the impression that you're telling me something I don't know, Kelsey? I don't have that short a memory, sweetheart."

Kelsey hadn't meant to sound insulting. Because her mother was with her, she slowed down rather than raced through a yellow light. "No, of course not, it's just that—that I'm worried."

Kate patted her hand just as the light turned green again. "Don't be. This baby thing threw me for a loop, too, but I'm already getting used to it. It'll mean changes, but it'll also mean that I get to hear a sweet little voice say 'Mama' again."

"I can call you Mama again if you want," Kelsey volunteered as she took the on-ramp to the northbound freeway. "What about the diapers and the sleepless nights and the cost?"

In Kate's mind, the reward was a great deal more than the sacrifice. "What about the love?" she countered.

Kelsey spared her mother a quizzical glance. "Five of us loving you—not counting Dad—isn't enough?"

Her mother's laugh was warm, reassuring, as if she sensed the ambivalent feelings Kelsey was going through.

"There's always room for more, Kelsey. *Always*

room for more. A mother's love is infinite. It's not a pie with only so much to go around so that if you slice it seven ways instead of six, there'll be less for everyone." Kate shifted in her seat for a better view of her daughter. "I'll still love everyone the same way, Kelsey. There'll just be one more at the table, that's all."

She was grateful to her mother for not saying that this was ultimately not her business to meddle in. But then, both her parents had made all of them feel that they were a unit, not parents and children or worse, individual strangers. In her family's case, although individuality was encouraged, at bottom it was a case of one for all, all for one.

And she needed to get behind this newest phase, Kelsey told herself sternly.

There was sympathy in Kelsey's voice as she asked, "Then you're okay with this, Mom? With being pregnant, I mean?"

"I am *wonderful* with this," her mother assured her. Her eyes danced as she said, "Children keep you young."

For the first time since she'd rushed out of the school, Kelsey laughed. "I thought you said that children give you gray hair."

"That, too," Kate acknowledged. "But gray hair happens at any age. I had an aunt who started going gray at twenty-five. And the dividends are so wonderful. Look at you," she added to make her point.

"You're not afraid?" Kelsey asked, thinking of how she would have reacted if she were in her mother's shoes.

Kate let out a long breath. A great many emotions

shifted through her. Joy was foremost, but other emotions, as well. "I'm terrified."

"Terrified?" Kelsey looked at her, then back at the road. How could her mother be happy and terrified at the same time? "You certainly don't act it."

Kate was nothing if not honest. It was the cornerstone of her relationship with everyone in her family. That and love.

"Doesn't mean I'm not. The prospect of bringing a new life into the world is always terrifying. Will he or she be healthy? Will I do a good job raising him or her—"

Kelsey stopped her. "Seriously?" she asked incredulously.

"Seriously," Kate responded.

How could her mother possibly even spend half a second wondering? "Mom, you've got to be the world's greatest mother. You *know* that."

"What I might know and what the baby thinks are two very different things." Kate closed her eyes, momentarily slipping back into the past. "Remember when you packed up your storybooks and made a peanut butter and jelly sandwich, determined to run away from home because you were so angry at me?"

Kelsey had forgotten all about that until just now. The memory evoked a nostalgic laugh.

"I remember," she said with feeling. "You took Trevor's side against mine." She recalled how hurt she'd felt. Running away had been her only way to retaliate. She was convinced her mother would come searching for her, tears streaming down her face. After a sufficient amount of time, she would have forgiven her mother's transgression and returned.

God, had she *ever* been that young? Kelsey wondered.

"I mediated, I didn't take sides," Kate corrected. "And you were a little bully," she added with great affection. "You kept hitting him because you knew he wouldn't hit you back."

Kelsey shook her head. If anyone should have run away from home, it was her mother. "How did you put up with all that?"

The answer was simple. "Love makes everything easier to deal with."

"I guess," Kelsey murmured.

She'd never had that in her own life. Oh, she loved her parents and her brothers dearly, and she was even getting there with her new sisters-in-law. But as far as eventually having her own life partner, someone who would be there at her side until the end of time, Kelsey sincerely doubted that would ever happen.

At the moment, she was still working on trying to be okay with that scenario. So far she wasn't having all that much luck. But eventually, she'd get used to it, she promised herself.

Kate took a deep breath as Kelsey pulled the car up into the driveway. In a way, she was mentally bracing herself for what lay ahead. She turned to her daughter. "I'm counting on you to be there for me when I tell your father about the baby, you know."

"Wouldn't miss it for the world," Kelsey assured her,

turning off the ignition. "I'll bring the smelling salts."
She saw her mother looking at her, arching one very expressive eyebrow. "You've got to admit this is going to hit him like a bombshell."

"Not a bombshell," Kate protested, softening the description. "Maybe a little like getting caught in an unexpected summer downpour."

"If you say so. Hey, wait, let me help you," Kelsey cried as her mother opened the passenger door and began to get out.

"Kelsey, I'm perfectly able to—"

Her mother didn't get a chance to finish. Morgan had pulled his car up behind them and was now at the passenger side of Kelsey's vehicle. Placing his hand beneath her elbow, he was gently helping Kate out of the vehicle.

Kate smiled her gratitude as she gained her feet. "Thank you, Morgan."

"My pleasure, Kate."

He said it as if he meant it. What was the man's angle? Kelsey couldn't help wondering. Why was he being so accommodating?

"Once you're settled in," Morgan continued, "your daughter and I will get your car."

"You don't have to do this," Kelsey protested. She couldn't ask her brothers for help, but there were other people she could summon. "I've got friends I can call—"

"I'm sure you do," he said, cutting her off. "But I like seeing things through. It won't take long," he promised, addressing Kate again. "Besides, I'll be off duty soon."

Kelsey eyed him a little uncertainly. "I don't know much about being a cop," Kelsey admitted, "but don't you have to sign out or something?"

"Don't worry about 'or something,'" he told her. "I've got it covered. For all intents and purposes, I'm all yours."

Kelsey was about to quip "Lucky me" but stopped herself at the last minute when she realized that Morgan was no longer talking to her. Her mother was the recipient of the "I'm all yours" comment.

"This is all very nice of you," Kate protested, "but don't you have something else you should be doing?"

Morgan shook his head. "Not at the moment. This all comes under the heading of 'protect and serve.'" He slanted a look in her direction.

The man was obviously anxious to get going, Kelsey surmised. "Do you need anything before we go, Mom? Maybe you should lie down. I can take you up—"

Kate placed her hands on her daughter's shoulders. "I'm pregnant, Kelsey, not fragile. I'll be fine, trust me." Dropping her hands, Kate fished out a set of keys from her purse and held them out to her. "Here, you'll be needing these."

Kelsey merely smiled and accepted the keys. This wasn't the time to tell her mother that she knew how to hotwire a car, having learned how from one of the boys she'd dated while in high school. A boy who, once her brothers got wind of him and his reputation, never showed up at the house again. When it came to outsiders, her brothers had been fiercely protective of her. They still were.

"I'll be back soon, Mom," she promised, brushing a kiss against her mother's cheek.

"Don't forget, Kelsey, you're having dinner here tonight," Kate reminded her.

"Wild horses couldn't keep me away," Kelsey promised.

Kate turned toward the departing policeman. "You're invited, too, Morgan."

Kelsey stared at her mother, speechless.

The invitation took Morgan by surprise, as well. It was a couple of moments before he found his tongue. "Thanks, but I've got plans."

He hadn't, but in his judgment, this evening would be tough enough for the woman without making her husband share it with some total stranger.

Kate inclined her head, accepting his answer. "Some other time then, perhaps."

"Some other time," he echoed.

Morgan understood the worth of a line like that. It might have actually been uttered in the belief that "some other time" would happen, but he knew it wouldn't. The woman's gratitude, which had prompted her to tender the invitation in the first place, would quickly fade as she returned to her routine and the need to make the invitation a reality would fade along with it.

Still, it was a nice gesture, Morgan thought, following the attractive woman's equally attractive daughter outside.

"She's a nice woman, your mother," Morgan said, finally breaking the silence that had followed them into his squad car. The silence had spilled out throughout the vehicle and accompanied them for the first five minutes of the trip. It threatened to continue indefinitely.

"She is," Kelsey agreed. "Mom is one of a kind." She shifted in her seat, curious. "How long were you following her?"

Morgan glanced at her before looking back at the road. "Excuse me?"

"You said you saw her weaving erratically in the lane. How long were you following her? A minute? Two? Three?"

Morgan shrugged. "A minute, maybe two. I turned on Harvard where it intersected University Drive. Your mother had just driven by."

"And when you turned on your siren, she crashed into the bushes?" Kelsey asked.

Morgan knew where the young woman was going with this. She probably thought that his following her mother had made her nervous and that she'd hit the bushes because of him, not because she'd fainted. But Kelsey was wrong.

"I hadn't turned on my siren—or my lights yet," he added. He'd witnessed other accidents that hadn't turned out nearly as well. "All in all, your mother's a very lucky woman."

"Mom likes to call it the luck of the Irish," she told him.

His father's father had emigrated from Ireland when he was a boy. "Is your mother from there?"

"Why?" Kelsey asked guardedly.

"No reason. I just thought I detected a slight accent."

Periodically her mother tried to lose her accent, but her father always protested, saying he really loved the slight Irish lilt in her voice.

"The same could be said about you," Kelsey pointed out. "You're not from around here, are you?"

"No," he deadpanned, "I live in Tustin," he said, mentioning the name of the city next to Bedford.

She frowned. He was deliberately being obtuse. "That's not what I meant."

Morgan dropped the act. "I know what you meant, Ms. Marlowe. I'm from Georgia originally. Now do I get to ask a question?"

"As long as you understand that I don't have to answer if I don't want to." Her eyes met his. The ground rules were accepted. "Go ahead."

"Is this chip on your shoulder something recent," he asked amicably, "or is it some congenital thing?"

She opened her mouth to retort that it was none of his business *what* she had on her shoulder, but then she closed it again. She could almost hear her mother reprimanding her. And she'd be right. She was taking out her tension—and Dan's behavior—on Donnelly. Because he'd come to her mother's aid, he didn't deserve this.

"I'm sorry if I'm coming across a little testy—"

He laughed shortly. "*Little* being a relative term here," he interjected.

"Okay," Kelsey backtracked, "a lot testy," she admitted. "But nothing like this has ever happened to me before."

He glanced at her thoughtfully. "Correct me if I'm wrong, Ms. Marlowe, but 'this' didn't happen to you. It happened to your mother. She's the one you should be thinking about, not yourself."

"I *am* thinking about her. About how awful it would have been if she'd been hurt." She drew herself up, taking offense. "And just where do you get off lecturing me, Donnelly?"

"Not lecturing," he countered mildly, "just pointing the obvious out. Your mother's okay. A bit shaken up, but okay. That makes her one of the lucky ones."

Something in his voice caught her attention. Donnelly wasn't just spouting rhetoric, he was speaking from firsthand experience. Undoubtedly, as a policeman he'd seen things the average person hadn't, and they'd left a lasting impression. He was right. She had to take a page out of her mother's book and just focus on the positive.

Kelsey took a deep breath. She stared down at her hands. They were folded and clenched in her lap. She willed herself to relax as she tried to banish the tension gripping her.

"Yes, it does," she acknowledged. Kelsey knew she owed this policeman a debt for being so nice to her mother. A debt she didn't take lightly. "Listen, I'm sorry. I didn't even thank you for taking my mother to the hospital. You could have just called for an ambulance and gone on your way."

"No, I couldn't," he answered too quickly. When he caught the confused expression on her face, he tried to shrug away his near slip. "It's all part of that protect and serve thing I was telling you about. It's the job," he emphasized. Gratitude always made him feel awkward. He didn't know how to accept it or give it.

"Protect and serve," she repeated. "And which was this?"

A smile crept over his lips. A smile, she thought, that made him look more approachable. Not to mention sexy. She banished the last part from her mind. Policemen weren't sexy. If anything, they were trouble.

"A little of both," he answered.

With that, he turned the squad car onto University Drive. That was when she got her first glimpse of her mother's vehicle. From the rear, the car looked to be all right. But then they drew closer. And Kelsey saw the front of the vehicle. It definitely wasn't what she expected to find.

"Oh God," she cried without fully realizing it as Morgan got closer to the car.

It was *not* a pretty sight.

Chapter Four

The closer they came, the further Kelsey felt her heart sink. Although the back of her mother's car was untouched, the front was bruised, scratched and badly dented. If human, it would have easily been deemed the loser in a fight. She could just imagine what it was like under the hood.

Her mother's car held a very special place in her heart. She'd learned how to drive in it.

Kelsey could remember her mother sitting beside her while she practiced early in the morning in a deserted parking lot. She'd felt as if she was flying when in reality she was only going eleven miles an hour.

"Why didn't you tell me it was this bad?" she cried, staring at the vehicle.

Waiting until the road was clear, Morgan made a U-turn and guided the squad car directly behind the badly battered sedan. Kate's car had spun out before crashing into the bushes that ran along the perimeter of the college's athletic field.

By the time he opened his door, Kelsey had already left his squad car and was examining the damage to her mother's vehicle.

"To be honest, I didn't focus on the vehicle," he told her. "I was focused on making sure your mother was all right."

He had his priorities straight. And she was being waspish, Kelsey upbraided herself. Contrite, she nodded at him.

"Sorry. You're right. My mother definitely matters more than a mashed-up grill," she murmured, then circled around again to the front. The hood was pushed in, proving that the bushes were tougher than they looked. It was a miracle that her mother didn't sustain any bad cuts or bruises.

The driver's-side door creaked and groaned like an arthritic eighty-year-old man when she opened it. The door made even louder noises when she attempted to shut it again. It resisted complete closure.

Morgan nodded at the door. "Doesn't sound promising," he commented.

Sitting behind the wheel, Kelsey put her mother's key into the ignition and turned. The engine wheezed, then coughed and sputtered before finally giving up the ghost. With an exasperated sigh, Kelsey tried again. This time, the engine remained silent. There wasn't even a weak sputter. The third attempt was no better. Kelsey got out again.

"I'm going to have to call a tow truck," she sighed, resigned. She looked at him. "You have any recommendations?"

"Pop the hood."

He caught her by surprise. "What?"

"Pop the hood." He nodded toward the driver's side. "There should be a release right under—"

"I know where the release is," she told him. His assumption of her ignorance annoyed her. She wasn't one of those women whose entire knowledge about cars stopped at putting the key into the ignition.

Reaching into the car, Kelsey pulled the lever. The hood made a strange noise in response. It took Morgan a couple of minutes to free it from its latch.

"What are you doing?" she asked.

Morgan didn't answer her right away. He was busy assessing the damage and testing various connections, estimating what might be wrong with the car from the noises it had made—and some it conspicuously hadn't—when Kelsey had turned the key.

"Checking out the engine," he finally said just before she repeated her question. He dropped the hood back into place. "I know someone who's pretty much of a wizard when it comes to working on cars. I can get the car towed to his place."

"How much does this Mr. Wizard charge?" she asked.

Reaching inside the car, he removed the keys and handed them back to Kelsey. "He's reasonable."

"One man's reasonable is another man's steep," she pointed out, moving in front of him and getting into his face.

His eyes met hers. "Trust me, your mother will be all right with it."

Kelsey paused for a long moment, debating. Ordinarily, she would have given her mother the details and asked her what she wanted to do. But the woman had enough to deal with right now. And she supposed that a mechanic with a recommendation was better than trusting the fate of her mother's car's to the luck of the draw.

"Okay, give Mr. Wizard a call and ask him if he can come down to take a look at this."

There was just the smallest hint of a smile on the patrolman's lips. "Not necessary."

"What, you communicate with him by telepathy?" When he didn't answer, it suddenly hit her. "It's you?" she asked in surprise.

"My father ran a garage. I used to help out after school," he told her. "Turns out I had a knack for fixing things."

"So why did you become a policeman?"

Telling her that he didn't want to be like his father was far too intimate a revelation. Morgan merely looked at her for a long moment, then said, "Not all things that need fixing are cars."

From the way he said it, she had a feeling that Donnelly wasn't going to elaborate on the enigmatic statement even if she asked him to.

Her curiosity was instantly aroused.

Kelsey hated not knowing things, like the answer to

a question, the end of a story or the proper response to a riddle. She really needed to know. Once she found out the answer, the almost rabid desire to obtain a response vanished.

But for the moment, her curiosity had to take a backseat to getting her mother's car repaired. The sooner she finished up here, the sooner she could get back to the house. Her mother needed her. Needed moral support before breaking this news to the rest of the family.

Kelsey eyed the dormant vehicle. Did he intend to call a tow truck or attempt to levitate it? "So where do we go from here?"

Morgan thought for a moment, then said, "I've got an idea."

It was starting to feel like she had to drag everything out of him. "Which is?"

Instead of answering her he sat down behind the steering wheel and felt around on the left side of the steering column for the hood release. Pulling it, he got out and opened the hood again. This time, it sagged immediately, refusing to remain up long enough for him to test his theory.

"I need you," he said to Kelsey.

"Why, Officer Donnelly, we hardly know each other," Kelsey quipped, deliberately batting her eyelashes at him.

"Cute," he commented. "Don't get ahead of yourself. Come here."

Man's interpersonal skills left something to be desired, Kelsey thought. "Do I goose-step over," she asked, "or just shuffle?"

"Point taken." He hadn't meant to sound as if he was ordering her around. "Come here, *please.* I need you to hold up the hood while I try to get your mother's car going long enough to drive it over to my place."

Joining him, she put her hands under the hood and held it up for him. "Assuming that you can accomplish this mystifying feat, where will I be while you're driving the car?"

"You'll be the one who's driving the car," he corrected. "I'll follow in the squad car."

From where she stood, that didn't sound too promising. Kelsey stared down at the engine. "Is it safe?"

"To follow you?" he guessed, his expression unreadable. "I don't know yet."

"I was referring to driving the car."

"Well, we'll find out, won't we?" he quipped. And then he laughed at her surprised expression. "Don't worry, Kelsey. I won't put you in a car that's about to blow up." He went back to adjusting wires. "Too much paperwork to fill out if that happens."

She wasn't sure if he was pulling her leg or not. His expression certainly didn't enlighten her any. "Nice to know you have your priorities straight."

"I'll do just about anything to get out of doing paperwork," he told her absently as he experimented with another connection. Whatever he did seemed to please him. "Okay," he said, putting his hand up next to hers beneath the hood. "Put the key into the ignition again. See if it starts now."

Kelsey had grave doubts, but she did as he told her.

Turning the key, she began tapping on the accelerator, giving the car gas. The newer models were supposed to start up without that, but her mother's car had always been a bit temperamental.

On the third tap, the engine responded with a rumble that increased in strength.

"It's alive," she pronounced, imitating Dr. Frankenstein in the classic horror movie.

Instead of letting the hood fall the way he had last time, Morgan eased it down gently. "Whatever you do, don't turn it off. I want you to drive it over to my house," he reminded her.

"Not until you give me the address," she answered.

He'd forgotten about that. Morgan rattled off the address. "I'll be right behind you."

Kelsey hesitated. "Got a better idea. You lead the way, I'll follow. If the car dies, I'll honk the horn to let you know."

It made no difference to him which way they did it. He just thought she'd prefer to be out front, but her way would still allow him to call in without fear of losing sight of her. He needed to let dispatch know why he was going to be late getting the squad car back to the precinct.

"Okay," he nodded. "Give me a second."

Crossing back to the squad car, Morgan started the vehicle and then swung it around in front of her. It was time for her to play follow the leader, he thought, a smile curving his mouth.

* * *

"Where *were* you?" Kate asked when her daughter finally walked into the house.

"Busy playing musical cars with Officer Donnelly," Kelsey quipped. "First he took me to your car—it doesn't look happy," she confided. "Then I followed him to his house—"

"His house?" Kate did her best not to look pleased. Nothing put Kelsey off faster than when she believed she was being manipulated. Still, Kelsey could do a lot worse than the young officer.

Kelsey tossed down her purse and straddled the arm of the sofa. "Turns out he's a closet mechanic and will fix the car for you. He almost insisted on it. You created quite an impression on him, Mom," she said with a grin. "Anyway, then he brought me back here." Kelsey shrugged. "Not much of a story really." Her voice grew more serious as she appraised her mother. "How are you feeling?"

Kate ran her hand along her extremely flat stomach, trying to smooth down the unsettling churning.

"Like I'm going to throw up." She pressed her lips together, trying to think of other things.

Kelsey wondered if she should bring over a pail or the wastepaper basket from the kitchen. "I thought that only happened with first babies."

Kate took in a long, cleansing breath. She longed for some tea to settle her stomach. "Seeing as how it's been twenty-six years between pregnancies, this is practically like having a first baby."

"For the second time around," Kelsey commented. This whole thing was crazy, as if the world was somehow out of whack. And yet, there was this small, solid starburst of joy smack in the center of her being.

There was no denying it. She loved children almost as much as her mother did.

"But that's not why I feel like I'm going to throw up," Kate confided in a lowered voice, despite the fact that only the two of them were in the house.

"Oh?" And then Kelsey guessed what caused her mother's unease. "You're afraid of what Dad's going to say."

"Not say so much as feel," Kate admitted. She twisted her fingers together. "This is a lot to spring on him."

Kelsey had always been honest with her mother. She saw no reason to change now, even if this wasn't the easiest of subjects for a daughter to discuss with her mother.

"This is a lot to spring on all of us, Mom." Her mother looked a bit distressed. Kelsey quickly continued. "I mean, I know you guys love each other and all that, but I guess at this point in your married lives, I thought that your expressions of love were more or less restricted to holding hands and occasionally indulging in deep, soulful kisses."

Shaking her head in amusement, Kate ran her hands through the girl's hair. "Someday, my darling daughter, when your skin isn't quite as flawless as it is today, you'll come to realize the true meaning in that poem."

That had come completely out of left field. "What poem?"

"'Come grow old along with me, the best is yet to be,'" Kate said, reciting her favorite line out of a poem by Robert Browning. And then she patted Kelsey's hand. "Shouldn't you be getting back to school? I don't need a babysitter, honey."

"I'm not babysitting," she protested a bit too quickly. "I told them at the school I didn't know if I was going to be back today." And then she backtracked a little. "At least I think I did. Everything after talking to you on the phone is still a little hazy. Besides," she staked out a place on the sofa, "I thought I'd hang around here today, see if you need anything, need someone to catch you in case you faint again, things like that."

Kate took her daughter's hand and drew her up to her feet. "I'm fine, really. Go back to work."

Well, she *had* left them in a bad way. "If I didn't know any better, I'd say you were trying to get rid of me, Mom."

Kate grinned. She was gently guiding her daughter to the front door. "I am. I've changed my mind. I can handle this. Thank you for coming as quickly as you did—now go."

Kelsey paused in the doorway. She didn't want her mother to think she was hovering, but she didn't feel good about just leaving her. "You sure you don't need anything?"

Kate smiled. When she spoke, her accent was particularly strong. "Oh, a shot of my da's liquid courage, maybe." She reconsidered her words and gave Kelsey a rueful expression. "But then, I can't have that for the next nine months."

"Speaking of 'da,' when *are* you going to tell Dad?" Kelsey asked.

"Today," Kate answered. She'd already made up her mind. But suddenly weary, she took a deep breath. "I just have to find the right words."

"How about 'Hi, honey, I've got a new tax deduction for you'?"

Kate shook her head. "Very funny, Kelsey."

"I wasn't trying to be funny," Kelsey told her mother. "I was trying to temper the shock with a positive piece of information."

"He's not going to be in shock," Kate protested. But then her words echoed back to her. "He's going to be in shock, isn't he?"

"Can't really blame him, Mom. You were in shock when you found out," Kelsey reminded.

But that was different. "It was for just a few seconds."

"With luck," Kelsey deadpanned, "Dad'll come out of his shock just before he has to rush you into the delivery room." Kelsey leaned over and pressed a kiss to her mother's temple. "Just kidding, Mom. After he realizes you haven't just developed a weird sense of humor, he'll be thrilled."

Thrilled was a rather powerful word. "I don't know if I'd go that far…"

Kelsey gave her a vague little shrug. "Might as well keep a positive attitude about this." Reaching for the doorknob, she paused as a thought hit her. "Just make me a promise."

Raising five children had taught Kate never to make a promise until she heard all the details. "Yes?"

"Don't tell the guys without me there. I want to see their reaction. You can tell Dad," she realized they needed their privacy for this, "but not Mike and the others unless I'm there. Please," she added in case her mother didn't think she was serious.

"All right, I promise." Kate sighed and shook her head. "There's something decidedly fiendish about you at times, my darling daughter."

Kelsey gave her an innocent, angelic smile. "I don't know what you're talking about, Mom. See you in a few hours," she promised.

Once outside, Kelsey fought the very strong urge to call up one of her brothers. It didn't matter which one as long as she could tell one of them. She could almost feel the secret bubbling up inside of her, threatening to choke her.

Despite a fair amount of fighting between them when she was growing up and then again when she began dating, during which time they had taken it upon themselves to scare off every guy who came to the house, she and her brothers were close. Very close.

Moreover, there were no secrets in the family, except for perhaps when she was seeing Dan. But that had been done on the sly only because her brothers had been so hard on *any* guy she ever brought home.

So she hadn't told any of them, not even her mother, about Dan, and that had turned out even worse. In hindsight, she had no doubt that if her brothers had met the object of her young, foolish affections, one of them—most likely Trent—would have looked into Dan's background and found out that the patrolman was married. It would have hurt, of course, but less than when she'd accidentally found out for herself. By then, she'd given her heart away.

Reclaiming it, she'd gotten the organ back in little pieces, after which time she'd taken it off the market. But other than that, there were no secrets in her family, no continuing mysteries.

Kelsey eased the door closed behind her and went down the front walk.

This was going to knock all of them for a loop. She really hoped that her mother would opt to tell her brothers very, very soon because she really didn't know how long she could refrain from saying something or having something slip out. It wasn't that she couldn't keep a secret. Just that she knew her limitations. She couldn't keep a secret when it came to her family.

Reaching her car, Kelsey glanced over her shoulder at the house where she'd grown up and lived until recently. She was still in the process of moving her things from one place to another, but right now, she wasn't thinking about the outer trappings of her independence. She was thinking about her mother.

She wanted to remain with her mother, to care for her rather than the other way around. Her mother had selflessly been there for her, whether it was convenient or not. This was an instance when turnabout would only have been fair play.

But she had the feeling that her mother wanted to be

alone right now. To rehearse what she would say to her father when he came home. And to maybe get used to this huge curveball life had thrown her. Granted her mother loved babies, but despite her protests, this *had* to be difficult to accept.

This wasn't like picking out new wallpaper for the downstairs powder room. This had lasting repercussions.

Life, the way her parents knew it, had changed forever.

But she supposed that her mother was right. She needed to get back to work and let the dust on this settle.

A baby.

Who would have thought it?

Kelsey caught herself grinning as she drove back to her school.

Chapter Five

The briefcase slipped out of Bryan Marlowe's hand, falling to the floor with a *thwack*. He'd intended to place the briefcase next to the table by the front door, but Kate's unexpected announcement in response to his greeting had stopped him dead in his tracks and caused every muscle in his body to go lax.

The sound of the briefcase hitting the travertine floor jolted him back.

Shaking his head, Bryan bent down to pick up the fallen case. This time, he parked it beside the table.

As he straightened up again, Bryan flashed Kate a sheepish smile and quickly brushed his lips against hers.

"Sorry, Kate. I've had a rather rough day in court. Judge Wallace has to be the most adversarial judge on the bench these days," he sighed. "I actually thought I heard you say that you're—"

"Pregnant," Kate repeated quietly, finishing his sentence for him. She took a breath, not sure how to gauge his reaction. "You did. I am."

Like a man in a trance, Bryan stared at her. "You're sure?"

He was upset, Kate thought. Maybe she should have sprung this on him slowly. "The doctor is."

That surprised him, too. She hadn't said anything about going to the doctor today. Ordinarily, they shared little details like that, no matter how busy they were. "You've already been to the doctor?"

She nodded her head. "Not exactly voluntarily."

Kate paused for a moment, trying to find the best way to word this part of the narrative. There really wasn't a good way, so she simply forged ahead. She knew that some wives would have omitted this part or covered it up somehow. Husbands, at least husbands who cared as deeply as hers did, had a tendency to overdramatize in their heads a situation where bushes and crashing cars were involved. She didn't want to cause Bryan any anguish, but she could no more cover this up—or lie—to her husband than she could suddenly grow fins and dive down to the ocean floor.

She took another, deeper breath, then said, "I fainted."

Bryan instantly knew there was more to it than that. Searching her face, he put his hands on her arms to keep her in place. His eyes were on hers. "Where?"

Kate didn't try to look away. "In the car."

"You were driving?"

He'd actually gone pale. Maybe she shouldn't have been this truthful, Kate thought, regretting what he had to be going through. What she'd be going through if the tables were turned.

"Yes," she said in a small voice.

Bryan's hold on her arms tightened as her words sank in. His imagination took over. "Oh God, Kate, you could have been killed."

Kate glossed over that. Pointing out that she hadn't been killed wouldn't help. Instead, she gave him the details as succinctly as possible.

"I drove into the bushes. It happened on University Drive, just outside the college campus. I was on my way to work," she explained. "I fainted without any warning, just the way I had when I was first pregnant with Kelsey. But there was only that one time with her," she reminded him, hoping that would help to keep him from blowing the incident out of proportion and from fearing that there would be more fainting spells in the future. "And I'm fine now, really."

Bryan couldn't get himself to let go of her. After all these years of marriage, she was even more precious to him than ever. "You're sure?"

Sympathy filled her eyes. "Bryan, when have I ever lied to you?"

"Never," he admitted. Trying to move past the vivid scene in his head, he took a deep breath. "A baby?"

Nodding, she smiled warmly. Maybe it wasn't going

to be so hard for him to accept this latest twist in their lives after all. "A baby."

Bryan let the information sink in. He knew he wasn't exactly at the best age to start all over again, but it was doable. "It's been a long time since we had one of those in the house," he said, his eyes meeting hers again. "I wonder if things have changed."

Kate laughed softly. "Not the basics. They still need to be fed and loved."

"And changed," he interjected, unconsciously wrinkling his nose as he said it.

"There's that, too," Kate allowed. And then she threaded her arms around his neck, just a wife with her husband, not a professional couple who had already raised five children. "Are you very disappointed?"

"Disappointed?" he echoed, puzzled as he encircled her waist with his arms and held her closer to him. "Why would I be disappointed? It's not like I asked for a pony and got this instead."

Laughing, Kate shook her head. "No, I mean, well, you talked about traveling…" He'd mentioned early retirement once or twice and the plans he had for their future.

To allay her fears, Bryan stole a quick kiss. "That's all that it was, Kate, just talk. Despite my occasional grumbling—like today—I like what I do. I really don't want to retire." His eyes skimmed over his wife's very trim form. "And now I have a reason not to," he quipped. "Have you seen what college tuitions have gone up to these days?"

Kate pressed her hands against his chest, as if to stop

his flow of words. "Wait, wait, the baby's not even born yet. I think we can hold off for a while before getting him or her enrolled in college."

The news—and the changes it was going to cause in their world—was still sinking in. And he was happy. Having another baby might be interesting.

"It'll be happening before you know it." Bryan framed her face with his hands. "I love you, Mrs. Marlowe."

"And I love you, Mr. Marlowe," Kate echoed back just before her husband kissed her warmly and deeply. She leaned into him, absorbing every nuance with every fiber of her being, her soul lighting up.

Which is how Kelsey found them a minute later as she let herself in with her house key.

"Hey, break it up, you two," she chided, pocketing her keys. "That's how you got into this mess in the first place."

Kate was still holding on to her husband's waist as she shifted slightly to face their daughter.

"It's not a mess, Kelsey," Bryan protested and then he stopped, surprised. "She knows?" he asked Kate.

Kate nodded. "I called her from the hospital," she confessed.

She could see that the news stung him a little. "Her and not me?"

Kate rested her head against his shoulder, relief and comfort setting in. "You had a big case in court today. You told me that last night. I wasn't about to draw your focus away from that. If I'd called to tell you I was in an accident, you would have dropped everything and come running. Clients don't appreciate that," she reminded him.

"Okay, I'll accept that. What's your excuse?" Bryan turned toward Kelsey. "Why didn't you call me when you found out?"

Kelsey pointed to her mother. "She made me promise not to tell."

Bryan extrapolated on the information. "Your brothers don't know?"

Kelsey shook her head. "Not yet." She slanted a look at her mother. "And believe me, it was *not* easy not picking up a phone and calling them."

Kate's smile filled the room as she patted her daughter's arm. "I appreciate you keeping your word, Kelsey."

Kelsey nodded, dismissing the thanks. "Sure. Can I call them now?" she wanted to know.

"All right. Call them and invite them to dinner for tomorrow night," her mother instructed. "I think we should tell all four of them at once." She smiled as she glanced at Bryan. "The way we did when we told them you were marrying their nanny."

Bryan laughed. "Best decision I ever made, not counting talking you into *being* their nanny."

A widower, he'd been at his wit's end at the time, after having lost not one but three nannies in a short amount of time because his sons had proved to be far too energetic for any of the women to handle. Kate had been a college student when they'd met. She was studying child psychology and piecing together odd jobs to earn enough money to keep herself eating and in college. He'd glimpsed her at a birthday party his oldest, Mike, was attending. Kate had been hired to provide the entertainment. She did so by bringing the puppets she'd brought with her to life.

Watching her, Mike had been mesmerized and he, Bryan later realized, had been captivated. He, and more importantly a rent hike in Kate's apartment complex at the time, convinced her to come to work for him as a live-in nanny.

Not a day went by when he wasn't grateful that things had turned out the way they had.

"I have to wait a whole day before I can tell them?" Kelsey complained.

"Afraid so," Bryan said. "It's your mother's announcement to make. For now, this can stay our little secret," he added with a wink. "It'll give you something to lord over your brothers later."

"Where's the car, Kelsey?" Kate suddenly asked.

Kelsey was about to remind her mother that she'd already told her where the car was, but decided not to belabor the point. Her mother was dealing with a lot here. She could be forgiven a little forgetfulness.

"It's over at Morgan's house," she answered, then, just in case her mother had forgotten this part, too, she added, "He said he was going to work on it."

"Oh, that's right." Her mother seemed a bit chagrined. "You already told me that. Sorry, I'm still a little scattered, I guess."

Bryan looked from his daughter to his wife. "Morgan?" he repeated.

"Morgan Donnelly," Kelsey told him. "He's the policeman who took Mom to the hospital."

Obviously there was more to the story than he'd heard. Bryan stared at his wife, wide-eyed. "Police were involved?"

"Just the one," Kate answered, holding up a single finger.

Taking her hand, Bryan drew her over to the sofa and sat down, urging her to take a seat beside him. "Maybe you'd better tell me the rest of it. From the top," he prodded.

"Wouldn't mind hearing it in order myself," Kelsey agreed, taking a seat opposite her parents on the recliner.

"There's not that much of a story," Kate pointed out. When they continued looking at her, she nodded. "Okay, from the top, then," she said, beginning her narrative.

Morgan juggled cars when he came home from the precinct, moving Kate's car into his garage and leaving his own parked outside. The weatherman had predicted rain—not that he believed it for a minute. This was just barely autumn and their rainy season didn't start until November—if it decided to show up at all. But it was always better to be safe than sorry. And he'd had enough of "sorry" to last him a lifetime.

Stopping at a fast food drive-through, Morgan brought home his usual dinner: burger and fries accompanied by a large soda. He carried the fast food into the garage, intending to eat while he worked. The reception on his secondhand radio was clear tonight, left alone by the static gods that usually plagued it. Music filled up the quiet and it helped. Some.

Leaving the garage door opened, Morgan went to the wall of tools to select the ones he would need, at least to get started.

Technically, they were his tools because there was no one left to own them, but in his mind they were and always would be his father's tools. Six months after his father's funeral—and the grand jury inquisition that had cleared Morgan of all blame—he'd sold the house where he'd grown up along with his own home and moved out here. Georgia was filled with too many memories for him, haunting memories, and he wanted a fresh start, away from the pain.

He would never have been able to move on if he'd stayed in Georgia. Too many familiar places, too many ghosts to deal with. And, although some of the memories were good, the others were just too painful. So he'd come out here to start fresh.

Except that he didn't start. He just continued. Continued being a cop because that was what he did best. Continued being a man without a family because his had died on him—by choice or otherwise.

He'd told himself that he had made his peace with that, but he hadn't. Not yet. For now, it was still a work in progress. He had his good days and his bad. If he was lucky, they balanced out.

Taking a wrench from its designated space on the wall, Morgan held it for a second. He could have sworn it was still warm from his father's hand, except that his father hadn't handled any of the tools in more than three years. Not since he'd lost the use of his legs.

Morgan stared at the socket wrench, thinking.

In a way, he supposed that he understood. Understood why his father had opted to lose himself in alcohol after his mother had died of leukemia. Alcohol did numb the pain. But then, as its effects wore off, the pain only seemed greater and more overwhelming in comparison. And because of what he'd seen alcohol do to his father, taking away his strength, his identity and, finally, his legs thanks to the stroke, Morgan was determined not to use alcohol like a crutch, as his father had.

Although God knew he had reason to.

He walked over to the vehicle he had volunteered to fix. On nights like this, when for some reason memories of Beth and Amy, his wife and daughter, seemed even more vivid than usual, Morgan found himself longing for something to numb him, to either vanquish the pain or knock him out.

But he wasn't going to risk losing his self-respect, not to mention the use of body parts, the way his father had. Drinking himself into oblivion only led to a dead end and to further despair. For whatever it was worth, he was glad this "project" had fallen into his lap. Glad for the diversion working on the vehicle provided him.

Marvin Gaye lamented the impending departure of a girlfriend and that he'd heard about it not from her, but through the grapevine as Morgan rolled up his sleeves and got started.

All in all, her father had taken the news a lot better than she'd anticipated.

He was a very flexible man, her father. Growing up, he'd been an immense comfort and her ally against her brothers. She'd always thought that he doted on her because she was his only girl.

That might not be the case in another eight months or so.

How did she feel about that? she asked herself as she drove home. She knew that as they were growing up, her brothers had thought she was spoiled, but she wasn't. Although she'd always liked the idea of being the only girl, she was an adult now. Her priorities had changed. She found herself hoping that the baby *would* be a girl. It would give her father someone new to worry about and take the focus off her life.

Not that much was going on in her life right now. But there would be, when she decided to get back into the swing of things again. This time she wouldn't have to worry about a man being interrogated by her father or one of her brothers.

Freedom.

She could almost smell it.

Whistling, Kelsey was just pulling into her residential complex when her cell phone started melodically playing one of her ring tones.

Kelsey let her phone ring one more time as she drove into her parking space. Pulling up the hand brake, she turned off the ignition. Only then did she take out her cell phone. Because the call wasn't coming from anyone in her family, she felt no sense of urgency to answer.

"Hello?"

"Thought I'd give you an update."

The deep male voice undulated into her nervous system, sending it into high alert. "Morgan?"

"Sorry. Guess I should have identified myself first."

"No need for that," she told him. "You have a very distinctive voice."

Once she recognized his voice, she couldn't understand why it had taken her even a minute to make the connection. Donnelly's voice was deep, basement-cellar deep, and rumbled slightly as he spoke.

When she'd given him her phone number in case he needed to run something about the car by her, she hadn't expected to hear from him so soon. Holding the cell phone against her ear, Kelsey made herself comfortable in her seat and got down to the heart of the matter.

"Is this going to be a good update or a bad one?" she asked.

"Good, actually." His voice shifted, as did the quality of the phone's reception. She assumed he was moving around as he spoke. She thought she heard the sound of traffic in the background. Or was that music? "It's not going to take me as long as I thought to fix the car."

"Inside and out?" she asked. Just how fast could this man work? Didn't he have a life outside his job?

"Inside," Morgan specified. "The body work might take me a little longer."

She heard what sounded like something hard and metallic hitting the floor. He was calling from his garage, she surmised.

"You do body work, too?" She didn't bother hiding the admiration in her voice.

"Like I said, my father ran a full-service garage," Morgan explained. "He prided himself on doing everything a vehicle owner might need. He considered himself not just a mechanic, but an artist."

He was referring to his father in the past tense. Did that mean the man was dead, or just no longer working?

Kelsey squelched her natural desire to ask for details. If Donnelly wanted her to know about his father, he'd tell her on his own. Until then, it was none of her business. Even as she told herself that, she remembered how much she'd always hated that phrase. It was like a huge hurdle for her, getting in the way of her finding things out.

"I want you to keep track of everything," she told him. "My mother is going to want to pay you when you're finished."

There was silence on the other end, and for a second she thought that maybe her phone had cut out and he hadn't heard her. "I said—"

"I heard you," he said, cutting her off. "Not doing it for the money."

He'd almost snapped that at her. *You're a strange man, Officer Donnelly.* Out loud she asked, "What are you doing it for?"

Again there was silence. Either he hadn't heard her, or he was debating whether or not to answer her. Finally, he said, "To keep busy."

She would have thought that he wanted just to unwind with a beer, watching some mindless show on TV.

"What, police work doesn't take up enough of your time?"

More silence. She began to feel as if the only way to converse with the man was to drag the words out of him. Did he forget that he was the one who'd called her?

And then he finally deigned to give her a response. "No."

She'd meant it as a joke. He, apparently, wasn't taking it that way. He sounded completely serious.

Just who was this guardian angel with semitarnished wings? And why did he feel he needed to keep busy? To keep from thinking? About what?

Just what was Donnelly running from? she couldn't help wondering.

Chapter Six

The following evening, as they waited in the family room, Trevor Marlowe looked from one sibling to another.

From what he could see, no one seemed any more enlightened than he was. But it never hurt to ask. "Anybody know why Kate made a point of gathering us all here tonight?"

"When Kelsey called," Trent told him, "all she said was that Kate wanted to see us."

"That's what she said when she called us," Travis put in, nodding toward his fiancée, Shana.

All four brothers exchanged looks. Each was in the dark. And they didn't like it.

Trevor frowned. It was obvious that *something* was up.

"Maybe she finally found out who went through the

box of pictures she used to keep hidden in the back of her closet." Mike eyed Trent pointedly.

Trent had been the one who, years ago, had come across faded photos of a high school beauty in a bikini. Mike had been the one to see the resemblance between the girl and Kate. It had been the one secret they'd kept from their stepmother. At the time, it had been "big stuff," at least in their very young opinions.

"And what, she decided to gather us all together like that funny little Agatha Christie detective?" Trent asked, his tone dismissing Mike's suggestion as absurd. "You know who I mean. The Belgian guy with the waxed moustache."

Travis's curiosity was as aroused as the rest of them. He laughed shortly at Trent's comment. "We hardly ever know what you mean, Trent. You're a psychologist. Psychologists have their own way of looking at things."

"The point is, Kate wouldn't be this dramatic over something like that," Trent insisted. Just then, Kelsey walked into the room.

The brothers instantly closed ranks around their sister, with Mike pouncing on her first. "How about you, Kelse? You have any idea why Kate wanted to see all of us at the same time like this?"

"You don't think she's ill, do you?" Venus, Trevor's wife, asked, concerned.

The least she could do was dispel that worry for them, Kelsey thought. "No, Mom's not ill." The others watched her as if they expected her to further enlighten

them. It was absolutely hell holding her tongue.
"Maybe she just misses you," Kelsey added with a
careless shrug.

Get out here, Mom, she silently begged, glancing
toward the doorway that led into the dining room. *I
don't know how much longer I can go on pretending I
don't know anything.*

"Why would she miss me?" Trent asked. "I work in
the same office. She sees me every day," he reminded
Kelsey. It was because of Kate that he had gone into
child psychology in the first place, and when he got his
degree, she brought him into the practice with two other
psychologists.

Studying his sister as she spoke, Mike suddenly
nodded, as if giving credence to what he was thinking.
He watched Kelsey's reaction as he said, "You do know
what's going on, don't you?"

"Mike, don't badger your sister," Miranda chided,
coming to Kelsey's rescue. "If Kelsey knew, she'd tell us."

A sense of guilt mingled with relief. Grasping at straws,
Kelsey turned in Miranda's direction. "Have I ever thanked
you for marrying him and making him more civil?"

Miranda grinned at her. "I really can't take any credit
for that. Mike evolved very nicely all by himself."

Mike pretended to take offense. He would have
expected a show of a little more solidarity from Miranda. "What do you mean 'evolved'?" he asked.

Before either Miranda or Kelsey could offer an explanation, Kate came into the living room, bringing an
end to the speculation. Bryan was with her and they

were holding hands, presenting the same united front they always had while guiding their children through the various perplexing twists and turns.

Travis was the first on his feet. "What's going on, Dad?" he asked. Like his father, he was a lawyer, practicing at the same firm. He thought, if something was going on, that he would have picked up some telltale signs earlier today when they'd conferred about one of the firm's cases. But there hadn't been any indication of a problem.

Was something wrong? Or were they all just jumping to conclusions because life had been so good for so long and everything must come to an end eventually? None of them were so short-sighted that they had forgotten what it felt like to lose their birth mother.

"Does this have anything to do with the fact that you weren't in yesterday?" Trent asked, suddenly remembering that she'd been vague when she'd called in.

Kate smiled serenely at Trent as she sat down on the sofa. "Yes."

A small, sudden intake of breath closely resembling a gasp came from Venus. "You're pregnant," Trevor's wife cried. She looked as surprised as the others were to hear the words when she realized that she'd said them out loud. Venus quickly covered her mouth.

"Honey, don't be silly, Kate's not—" Trevor's protest faded away as he glanced at the woman he and his brothers had adored almost from the first moment she'd come into their lives. His jaw dropped open as the protest died on his lips. "You're kidding."

Quickly, her stepsons all moved in closer. "Kate?" Mike asked uncertainly.

Kate laughed softly, shaking her head. "So much for a dramatic announcement," she said with an amused sigh. "I should have known I couldn't keep anything from you boys for long."

"Long?" Travis echoed Kate's last word. "How long have you known you were expecting, Kate?"

"Not long. Just since yesterday. I had a little incident—" Kate lifted her shoulders slightly, dismissing it before she gave any details.

Her stepsons exchanged looks. They all knew how she tended to minimize things when it came to her own life. "What kind of an 'incident'?" Trevor asked, concerned.

When Kate didn't reply immediately, Kelsey answered for her, ending any escalating speculation on their part. "Mom fainted."

"In the house?" Laurel was the first to ask.

"She wouldn't have called it an 'incident' if it was in the house," Trent said with conviction, looking at his stepmother. "Would you, Kate?"

"She fainted in the car," Kelsey answered.

"Kelsey," Kate chided. She was hoping to keep that from them. It was bad enough that Bryan knew.

"They've got a right to know, Mom," Kelsey pointed out. If she was the one in the dark, she would have wanted to know, she reasoned.

All four of her half-brothers, as well as their wives and Travis's fiancée, drew even closer, as if to physically protect Kate.

"In the car?" Mike echoed, horrified. "Kate, you could have been—"

Kate cut him off. There was absolutely no reason to go there or torture himself with what *could* have happened. She didn't believe in speculation that left a person tortured.

"But I wasn't. I didn't even get a bump on the head." To prove it, she pushed back her bangs, exposing her forehead to Mike's scrutiny. "One of Bedford's finest was driving right behind me and he insisted on taking me to the hospital."

"Which reminds me," Bryan said. "I want to meet this police officer. I need to personally thank him for taking care of you."

"Kelsey knows where he lives. She can get in contact with him and invite Officer Donnelly to dinner," Kate told him.

Which brought everyone's focus back to a small but vital piece of information that had temporarily been pushed aside. Mike held up his hand, bringing the conversation to a temporary stop.

"Hold it. Let me get this straight." He spared his sister a glance before asking Kate, "Kelsey *knew* you were in the hospital and that you'd fainted?"

"Of course she knew," Trevor said impatiently, feeling just a little betrayed. "She just said Kate fainted."

Mike turned to his sister. "And when you called us to invite us over for dinner tonight, you knew Kate was pregnant?"

This was where lying would really come in handy,

Kelsey thought. But she opted to go with the truth. In the long run, it was for the best. Keeping the secret hadn't been her idea anyway. "Yes."

Travis, Trent and Trevor were triplets and inclined, at times, to share the same thought. This was no exception as they simultaneously cried accusingly, "You knew and you didn't tell anybody?"

Kelsey held the truth up as a shield. "Not by choice. Mom asked me not to."

Mike shook his head, stunned by both the news and the fact that Kelsey had kept it from them. "Doesn't matter. Since when could you *ever* keep a secret? You're like a sieve. Secret goes in, secret comes out almost immediately."

Kelsey lifted her chin defensively. "There're a lot of things about me that you don't know," she sniffed.

Closing her fingers around her husband's hand, Kate raised her voice to be heard above the growing din. "Boys, I didn't have Kelsey call all of you here to listen to you argue. This is time for a celebration—"

"Celebration? Why don't we hold off for a while? The baby might turn out to be another Kelsey," Trent pretended to protest. It got him a swat to the back of his head from his sister.

When Trent turned to his wife for comfort, Laurel raised her hands in protest. "Don't look at me. I'm on her side."

"Face it, guys," Kelsey said cheerfully. "We finally outnumber you."

Travis addressed his stepmother. "I vote for a boy."

"Me, too," Trent and Trevor chimed in.

Mike raised his hand in the air. "Ditto."

Kate laughed. "Sorry, boys, I'm afraid that it doesn't work that way." She glanced at her daughters-in-law and Shana. "Maybe your ladies can explain it to you later."

"Or better yet, show us," Trevor suggested, nuzzling Venus.

"Later," Bryan suggested firmly, then rose to his feet, bringing Kate up along with him. "C'mon, guys, dinner's getting cold. Let's take this discussion to the dining room," he urged, leading the way.

"What did you make, Kate?" Trevor asked, ushering Venus before him. More than anyone, Kate was responsible for his pursuing his love of cooking and getting a restaurant of his own.

"Not me," Kate said, slipping her arm around Kelsey's waist. "Kelsey wanted to make dinner."

"Oh God," Travis groaned, rolling his eyes. "Get out the stomach pump."

Kelsey looked at his fiancée. "Shana, you want to hit him, or should I?"

"We're not married yet," Shana reminded her. "You can do it."

"If you insist," Kelsey said, grinning just before she smacked Travis upside his head.

The day felt as if it had gone into a sudden death play-off, lasting way too long. Morgan had been involved in a two-hour car chase in pursuit of a stolen vehicle. It had ended badly, with the carjacker crashing the stolen car into another car. The driver of the second car had been thrown and was in critical condition, while the carjacker had gotten himself all but permanently sealed in the crumpled front seat.

When the fire department came on the scene, they had to use the Jaws of Life to extract the carjacker. The man had screamed the entire time. Once freed, he'd been taken to the hospital in a second ambulance.

The felon looked far too young to buy the alcohol emanating from his pores. Unlike the innocent driver he'd hit, the carjacker was conscious and cursing a blue streak as he was taken away to the hospital.

How did people get to be so stupid? Morgan couldn't help wondering as he hung a work lamp on the inside of the hood of Kate Marlowe's car. Moving it over a fraction, he managed to maximize the beam of light.

He'd just finished fiddling with the lamp when he heard a car approaching. It slowed down then stopped right before his house. Morgan reached for the weapon he'd laid down next to his tools.

Getting out of her vehicle, Kelsey found herself looking down the barrel of a service revolver. Survival instincts had her instantly raising her hands over her head. She took a tentative step forward. Slowly.

"I didn't realize I had to ask for permission to approach."

What was she doing here? Morgan put the safety back on his weapon. "Sorry," he apologized, his tone flat as he put his gun back down on the counter. "Wasn't expecting you."

"Who were you expecting?" she asked, eyeing the weapon. "Some thug with a grudge?"

He picked up a wrench. "Let's just say that I like to be cautious."

"O-kay," she allowed, stretching the single word out as far as it could go.

"What are you doing here?" he asked as he returned to work on the vehicle. He'd replaced a number of damaged hoses yesterday and wanted to be sure they were all carefully tightened. "Checking up on your mother's car?"

It was as good an excuse as any, she thought, working her way up to the real reason she was here. "Sort of."

He wasn't used to having anyone stop by.

Beth would have been inviting her to dinner, he thought. She always cooked more than they could eat in a single sitting. But all he had were the remnants of his fast food order. He sincerely doubted that Kelsey would be interested in splitting.

"Want something to drink?" he finally offered. "I've got soda and beer."

"I'm fine," Kelsey told him. "But thanks for offering." She ran the tip of her tongue along her lips. Now or never. He'd already turned her mother down once, so what did she have to lose? "Speaking of which—"

He raised an eyebrow. "Yes?"

Kelsey cleared her voice. The words rushed out. "My mother sent me here to offer you an invitation to dinner tomorrow night." She held up her hands in case he was going to turn her down. She'd already made up her mind not to take no for an answer. "Actually, it's my father's idea. Not that she wouldn't have tried to invite you a second time herself—it's just that I think she's busy trying to process the fact that she's going to have a baby."

Morgan set down the wrench he was holding and looked at her. "Why would your father want to invite me over?" The Marlowe home was located in Spyglass Hill. The people who lived in Spyglass Hill didn't rub elbows with people from his side of town.

"To say thank-you for saving his wife in person," she told him simply.

"Your father could just show up at the precinct if he wanted to do that."

"My dad doesn't believe in doing things in half measures," she informed him. "Not since he married Mom. From what I'm told by my brothers, she taught him how to seize life with both hands and embrace it." But they were getting away from the immediate subject. "So, are you free?" she asked.

As a rule, he went out of his way not to fraternize with people. "People" included the men and women on the job and his neighbors. The latter group had tried to get him to come to a barbecue and a birthday party. After two refusals, neighbors stopped trying.

He liked it that way. Morgan had made his peace with facing day-to-day life away from the force as a solitary man. He kept his head high and his expectations low. That way he wasn't caught unaware or disappointed.

But Kelsey was a different story entirely. She continued looking at him expectantly. She might have gone on like that indefinitely, he realized. He finally shrugged his shoulders and said yes to get rid of her. "Okay. Yes, I guess so."

"Good." She moved on to the next step. "Mom wanted me to ask you what your favorite meal is."

He laughed shortly, adjusting one of the belts. "Anything that microwaves in less than five minutes."

Watching him work, Kelsey shook her head. "I think she was referring to a real meal, Officer Donnelly."

It had been a very long time since he'd found himself facing a real meal. Morgan raised his eyes from the inside of the engine and looked at her. "I don't know. Surprise me."

I want to, Morgan Donnelly, Kelsey caught herself thinking as heat rushed up and down her body.

But, because her mother expected some feedback, Kelsey pressed. "No, really. Pot roast, lasagna, chicken parmesan, name it. My parents really want to show you how much they appreciate you going out of your way."

He said something under his breath that she didn't catch, other than "good deed" and "punished." "Just doing my job," he told her dismissively. "It's part of the job description."

"You hung around at the hospital to see how my mother was doing and you're working on her car right now. As far as I know, that doesn't come under anything that can be found in the police procedure manual."

After hours, dressed as a civilian, he found that he didn't work and play well with others. The uniform was his shield, something he could hide behind. Right now, he had no place to hide.

He'd already turned the Marlowe woman down once, he thought, annoyed. Why couldn't she just take no for an answer?

"This isn't necessary, you know," he told Kelsey, grinding out the words. "The invitation, dinner, not necessary," he repeated with feeling.

"I'm afraid it is as far as my dad's concerned. And you already know Mom wants you to come." She was losing ground and tried another approach. "Don't worry, you won't have to talk if you don't want to. There'll be plenty of people there to pick up the slack for you."

"Plenty of people?" Morgan questioned. He hadn't any desire to attend when he'd just assumed it was going to be just Kelsey and her parents. Now he *really* didn't want to accept the invitation.

Kelsey nodded. "Yes. My brothers and their wives. All except for Travis. He's just engaged but almost married. His fiancée will be there, too. And in Trent's case, his son."

"Brothers." Morgan rolled the word around in his mouth. When he'd been very young he'd wished for a brother or two to take the edge off his loneliness. He'd learned how to do that on his own. "How many do you have?"

"Too many," she quipped. Especially when they ganged up on her. But for the most part, she wouldn't have traded her life for anyone's. She paused, debating with herself if she should add the last part. "And I should tell you before you show up and it throws you—"

Morgan stopped trying to work and gave her his full

attention. He had no idea where she was going with this. "Throws me?"

"Yes. Three of my brothers are triplets." And then she replayed her words in her head and laughed. "Well, of course it would take three of them to be triplets. If there were only two, they'd be twins. Anyway, Trent, Travis and Trevor take some getting used to before you can tell them apart. It's a little overwhelming at first, but it can be done," she assured him.

She made it sound as if it would be more than a one-time event. He wasn't sure if he could stand even one dinner. For now, he didn't argue. "You said three of your brothers, so how many do you have?" he repeated.

"Just four." Her own words amused her. There was no "just" when it came to her brothers, especially when she thought back to the years when they were growing up. But she didn't want to rattle Donnelly. "And they're all decent guys—just don't tell them I said so."

He had no intention of spilling to her brothers because, more than likely, he wouldn't be meeting them. But then he had a nagging feeling that if he protested, the perky woman before him with the dancing, bright blue eyes and the torrent of golden-blond hair would launch into some kind of frontal attack until he surrendered.

So, for the sake of peace, he nodded. "No problem."

Morgan hadn't counted on the Marlowe woman being able to read body language. "Oh, there's a problem, all right," she said.

Kelsey's tone aroused his curiosity. "What do you mean?"

She looked at him knowingly. He realized he wasn't dealing with some empty-headed, fluffy little blonde. There were brains inside that head of hers.

"You're not planning to go, are you?" She didn't give him a chance to deny it. "Morgan, my mother doesn't ask for much. Most of the time she's busy making sure all of us have what we need. I don't want to see her disappointed. If she wants you at dinner, then you'll be at dinner," Kelsey said with finality. "It's as simple as that."

Oh, is it, now? "You realize that threatening a policeman is against the law."

"No threats," she said innocently, spreading her hands wide to emphasize her point. "Just a friendly nudge in the right direction. Now, is six o'clock okay with you?"

He shrugged. Maybe he'd go and maybe he wouldn't. He'd see about what he'd do tomorrow. "As good a time as any."

"Good, now that that's settled," she brightened considerably as she moved in closer beside him and faced the exposed engine, "tell me what you're doing."

He tried not to notice that her perfume seemed to fill his senses. "You're a car junkie?" he asked.

Her smile was as sunny as her mother's. "I wouldn't put it that way, but I'm always open to learning something new."

He had this unsettling feeling that she had just promised him something.

Chapter Seven

He was *not* looking forward to this.

But the same gut feeling that warned him of danger on the job told him that if he didn't put in an appearance at the Marlowes', the younger Marlowe woman would show up on his doorstep again—and keep showing up until he made good on his promise.

They were right, he thought, tying his tie for the third time as he stared into the bathroom mirror. Those people who said that no good deed ever went unpunished, they were dead-on. What he should have done the other day was call the paramedics the second Kate Marlowe had driven her car into the bushes and let them handle the situation.

But he supposed that on some level he never got over

being a Boy Scout. And Boy Scouts didn't leave people, especially women, if they needed help. It was no more in him to have walked away from Kate than it was to walk away from a drowning man in the hopes that the next person on the scene would come to the man's rescue.

Still, his life would have remained simpler if he'd followed a different course....

Hindsight was a bear.

"You eat and you go. 'Hi'—chew—'goodbye,'" Morgan told his reflection with feeling. "With any luck, you'll be back here in a couple of hours."

The civilian looking back at him in the mirror appeared far from convinced that things would go that smoothly. Not with that little blonde with the flashing blue eyes as the wild card.

Maybe it was the clothes that were throwing him, Morgan thought, appraising himself carefully. He wasn't accustomed to wearing anything other than his uniform or jeans and a T-shirt in his off hours. Right now, he wore a light blue dress shirt—the only one he owned—the one he'd worn to Beth and Amy's funeral. The same could be said for his navy blue jacket. The only thing he had on that he'd worn in the last two and a half years were the light gray slacks.

When the tie still refused to come out right after a third attempt, Morgan muttered a curse, unknotted it and slid it off. With an exasperated sigh, he opened the top button in his shirt and left it that way. In his opinion, ties were only wasted pieces of fabric.

He glanced at his watch. It was just a little past five-thirty. The invitation was for six. He might as well get going, Morgan decided grudgingly. The sooner he got there, the sooner it would be over.

Instead of a comb, Morgan opted to run his fingers through his sandy-blond hair.

"Good enough," he pronounced, taking one last glance in the mirror.

A smudge on his shoulder momentarily stopped him in his tracks. He glanced down at his jacket and didn't see it, even when he put his thumb under the material and propped it up. Looking back at the mirror, he saw that the smudge had moved. It was closer to his chest now.

Morgan frowned. The smudge was on the mirror, not his jacket. With a shake of his head, Morgan made a mental note to clean the mirror when he got the chance. For the life of him, he couldn't remember the last time he'd cleaned it.

Considering the nature of his job, cleaning mirrors—cleaning anything within his house really—had rather a low priority on his list of things to take care of.

Muttering under his breath that this whole dinner thing was a complete waste of his time, Morgan walked out of the house, locking the door behind him.

A couple of hours, no more, he promised himself. It was a promise he intended to keep.

Kelsey glanced at her watch. He was late. Not by much, but he was late.

Maybe she should have gone to his place and

escorted him back to her parents' house. Not that she thought he'd lose his way—he was a policeman for heaven's sake, and they all came equipped with an inner GPS—it was just that she strongly suspected that he'd cop out at the last moment, no pun intended.

A watched door never opens.

With a sigh, Kelsey turned away from the door she'd been staring at for the past fifteen minutes, willing the doorbell to ring. She looked at her mother.

"Maybe we should just get started," she suggested.

"Give him a few more minutes, Kelsey," Kate urged pleasantly. "It's not as if Officer Donnelly has to clock in. He spends all of his time with rules and regulations, adhering to schedules. Maybe he likes to be lax when he's off duty."

Kelsey sincerely doubted that the man she'd talked to knew *how* to be lax. She had a feeling that he marched to his own drummer and didn't do anything he didn't want to do. At this point, she wouldn't have put any money on his showing up.

"You did tell him it was for tonight, right, Kelsey?" her father asked her.

"Absolutely," she answered. "I told him it was a command performance and if he didn't show up, I'd hunt him down and drag him back," she deadpanned.

"Bet that put the fear of God into him," Mike speculated.

Kate raised a reproving eyebrow as she looked at her daughter. "Kelsey—"

"She's kidding, Kate," Travis reassured his stepmother. "That's just her warped sense of humor—although," he winked at Mike, "I'd be pretty scared if I were him and she threatened me like that."

"You'd be scared if you caught your own shadow looming over you," Kelsey countered. "Like I said, we should all just start—" The doorbell rang. Kelsey did a complete about-face, spinning ninety degrees around on her heel to face the door. "I'll get it," she announced before anyone else had a chance to react.

Kate exchanged glances with Bryan. Her eyes crinkled as a knowing smile curved her mouth.

Bryan knew exactly what she was thinking. He hadn't been married to the woman all this time without picking up a few clues along the way. Kelsey was the last of their children to remain unattached, at least until the baby arrived. Kate wasn't going to be happy until Kelsey settled down with someone. Someone they deemed special enough for her.

Obviously, in Kate's eyes, this Officer Donnelly met the requirements.

Bryan bent his head and whispered in her ear. "Don't get your hopes up."

The look on Kate's face was the last word in wide-eyed innocence. "Why, Bryan, I don't know what you're talking about."

He knew better. "Yeah, right," he laughed.

Kelsey yanked open the door. She wasn't disappointed. "You came," she declared warmly.

Morgan glanced over her head to see a room full of people behind her. All looking in his direction. People who were probably going to expect him to make small talk. He didn't *make* small talk.

His gaze returned to Kelsey. "Did I have a choice?"

Her smile widened, traveling into her eyes, radiating from her face. Glad she could find humor in his discomfort, he thought grudgingly.

"No."

He snorted. "That's what I thought."

Kelsey lingered a moment longer. Her eyes slid over him. "You clean up nicely."

He met her compliment with a self-conscious, dismissive shrug. He grew even more self-conscious when a second look around made him realize that he was the only one in a jacket.

As if reading his mind, Kelsey offered a semi-apology. "I didn't think I had to tell you that it *wasn't* going to be formal."

Kate came to their rescue, greeting him warmly at the door with a quick hug that momentarily left him speechless. "Officer Donnelly, I'm so glad you could make it."

"Your daughter was very persuasive, ma'am," he replied.

"I believe the term is pushy," Bryan said. One hand on his wife's shoulder, he leaned forward and extended his right hand to the policeman. "Hi, I'm Kate's husband, Bryan. And I just wanted to thank you in person for taking such good care of my wife." Dropping his hand to his side, Bryan gave his wife a loving squeeze. "She means the world to me. To all of us," he amended, nodding toward the group of people behind him.

"Bryan, you're embarrassing me—" Kate chided, although she appeared far from embarrassed. "Not to mention that you're making Morgan uncomfortable."

When Kate Marlowe looked at him, Morgan immediately felt they were on the same wavelength. She seemed to be a down-to-earth, intuitive woman. He realized then that she reminded him a great deal of his own mother, not in her appearance, but in her manner, in her smile. It made enduring the evening a little easier.

"Let me introduce you to the motley crew behind you," Kelsey was saying. "As you've undoubtedly guessed by now, these are my brothers. The lovely, but for the most part clueless, ladies beside them are their wives—except for Shana who can still make a run for it if she comes to her senses."

Taking a fortifying breath, Kelsey began to recite all their names. "The guy who looks as if he's about to analyze you is Trent. He does that for a living. The woman beside him is his wife, Laurel, and that adorable little boy is their son, Cody. On Trent's left is Mike with his wife, Miranda. To *their* left are Trevor and Venus and Travis with Shana, who I've already introduced."

Finished, Kelsey looked back at Morgan and deadpanned, "Hope you were paying attention because there'll be a quiz at the end of the evening and you have to get a perfect score in order to be able to leave. Otherwise, we keep you here indefinitely."

He laughed shortly. "You're kidding." When she didn't confirm or deny his half-serious question, Morgan glanced over to the triplet closest to him. For the life of him, he couldn't remember the man's name. "She's kidding, right?"

"With Kelsey, you can never be sure," Travis answered with a straight face. "Here, you might find yourself needing this. I find that it helps." He placed a drink in the patrolman's hand.

Bryan picked it up from there, raising his own glass of wine high as he turned toward his wife. "To my beautiful wife, Kate," he toasted, "and the newest member of our family."

Morgan slanted what looked like an uneasy, confused glance toward Kelsey.

She almost laughed out loud. "He's talking about the baby," she said in case he thought he was being absorbed into the group.

"I knew that," Morgan answered with lips that barely moved.

The only one without a glass of wine in her hand, Kate threaded her arm through the young officer's.

"Come with me," she coaxed. "Dinner's about to get cold and there's nothing I dislike more than a cold dinner."

"I can think of a few things you dislike more," Mike offered mischievously, only to be poked in the ribs by his sister. "Hey," he protested. "What did you do that for?"

Rather than apologize or answer him, Kelsey glanced at his wife. "Sorry, didn't meant to usurp your position. Old habits are hard to break," she explained.

Miranda dismissed her sister-in-law's words with a wave of her hand. "Don't give it another thought," she told Kelsey.

Morgan didn't know what to make of the banter. It had been a long time since he'd been in any sort of company that remotely resembled a family setting. After his mother's untimely death, his father had completely retreated into himself, venturing out only long enough to buy more alcohol with which to drown his sorrows. For a while, desperate for a sense of family and afraid that his father was going to kill himself by inches, Morgan had tried his best to bring his father around. But the situation just grew progressively worse until his father's body rebelled against him and he had a stroke.

Morgan had been married at that point, with a brand-new baby, as well. Caring for his new family, working as a policeman and finding time to care for his father all but drained him. But for a while he managed to keep all the balls in the air.

They fell in short order, beginning with his father's suicide. The older Donnelly offed himself with his service revolver while he, Morgan, slept in the next room. After the inquest—he was acquitted—Morgan tried to get his life back on track. But life, quite obviously, hadn't felt like cooperating. Just when he had begun to entertain the hope that things were finally getting better, a drunk driver driving on the wrong side of the street in the middle of the day had extinguished all his hope in one fatal move.

Morgan had heard the report of the accident over his radio as dispatch called for the closest squad cars to get to the scene. He was instructed to help direct traffic until "the mess" could be cleared away. He hadn't a clue that the drunk driver's victims were his wife and daughter until he reached the area and saw the car he and Beth had picked out together in the middle of the intersection, bent and mangled practically beyond all recognition.

Paramedics had arrived several minutes before he had, and they were wheeling two gurneys by him. Both bodies were covered. Something about the small form beneath the sheet on the second gurney filled him with absolute fear. He stopped the paramedics and uncovered the body. A guttural cry of anguish rang in his ears as he raced to the first gurney and repeated the process. His partner later told him that the cry had come from him.

Morgan remembered his knees buckling. He remembered little else after that.

Beth and Amy, he was told, had both died instantly at first impact. And he, well, he had died by inches just like his father. A man couldn't survive too long when his heart had been cut out of his chest.

That was the last time he was in the company of a family.

All this, wrapped in numbing loneliness, crowded his brain and marched through his soul as he sat at the dining-room table, listening to Kelsey and the rest of them exchange barbs that were laced with thinly disguised affection.

He didn't belong here. The sooner he could leave, the better.

Intuitively feeling his discomfort and searching for a way to alleviate it, Kate inclined her head toward Morgan, who she'd placed next to her on her right.

"They can get a little overwhelming sometimes," she agreed, as if they had already discussed the subject at length.

Morgan looked at the woman who was responsible for his being here in the first place. Were his thoughts that transparent?

"It takes a little getting used to," she added. "But in the long run, it's well worth it. They're all very good people."

Catching the last of it, Mike turned to his stepmother. "That's because you made us that way." He glanced toward his father and grinned. "No offense meant, Dad."

Bryan laughed. "None taken." He regarded his guest and felt that an explanation was in order. "Before Kate came into our lives, I was completely at my wit's end with these guys. They were hell-raisers from the word *go*."

Morgan eyed Kelsey uncertainly as she gladly picked up the narrative. "Mom is actually their stepmother," she explained. "Dad initially hired her as a nanny. They had others before her, but legend has it that they kept dropping like flies—getting out of there the first chance they got."

"Hearsay," Travis protested. "Completely inadmissible in court."

"Total exaggeration," Trevor chimed in.

Mike laughed at his sister's description of the events. "You make it sound as if you were there, Kelse. You weren't even a gleam in Dad's eye."

Kelsey sniffed. "I've heard the story often enough to feel as if I lived through it," she informed Mike. "To hear Dad tell it, he was ready to run off and leave you guys without giving a forwarding address."

"The boys weren't that bad," Kate said, defending them. "They were going through a tough time, adjusting to life without their mother," she recalled, her heart filling with sympathy the way it always did when she recalled the first days she'd spent with her stepsons. "They were just a little too energetic for the average nanny—"

"Or any other non-superhuman being who crossed their path," Kelsey interjected.

"Do you have a family, Officer Donnelly?" Bryan asked, trying to head off another round of banter before it got out of hand.

He had a feeling that Kate had some very definite plans for Donnelly and he didn't want the young policeman to be entirely overwhelmed by his family. They were coming on rather strong. He knew that meant they were comfortable in Donnelly's company, but the officer might not understand that.

You would think that after more than two years, he wouldn't feel as if his insides were being skewered when he faced that question, Morgan thought.

"No," Morgan replied quietly but firmly.

"No family at all?" Cody's small voice had popped up out of nowhere. It was full of sympathy, as was his face when he looked up at the stranger.

Because the question had come from the lone child at the table, Morgan couldn't bring himself to be short, or to ignore the question outright, even though he wanted to. The wound was still too new, too raw, despite all the time that had gone by.

He doubted if it would ever be any different.

But the child was looking at him, his large eyes full of understanding that seemed far beyond his tender years. So Morgan confirmed what he'd said a moment ago. "No, no family at all," he echoed.

Out of the corner of his eye, Morgan saw the reaction on Kelsey's face. Her eyes were full of sorrow and the thing he hated most: pity.

It made him unaware that a rare thing had followed his answer. Silence was an unknown entity in the Marlowe household. But it came to the table now, if only for a moment.

Chapter Eight

A second later, the topic of conversation was deftly changed, shifting to something that everyone else at the table instinctively deemed would be a more neutral, comfortable subject for their guest.

"You like sports, Morgan?" Mike asked, falling back on the universal topic that most men—and a fair share of women—liked to expound on.

A vague shrug accompanied Morgan's response. "Depends on which sport you're talking about."

"Baseball," Miranda interjected, the subject being near and dear to her heart. In his day, her father had been a famous pitcher and had recently been inducted into the National Baseball Hall of Fame.

Because he occasionally followed the game when he

had a chance, Morgan replied in the affirmative. "Yeah, I like baseball."

Warming up to the subject, Bryan asked, "Angels or Dodgers?"

No passion was involved either way for Morgan, so he said, "Both."

"Well, then, you're in luck," Kelsey informed him. "Mike here writes a sports column." She flashed her oldest brother a quick smile. "He can get you tickets to any home game you want to see."

He didn't want anyone going out of their way for him. The tickets would most likely be wasted anyway. He had no burning desire to see a game in person.

Morgan shook his head. "Thanks, but I don't get much of a chance to attend games."

Kelsey looked at him in surprise. Who didn't like free tickets? Did he think they were trying to bribe him? If anything, it could be viewed as payment for his time spent on her mother's car.

"Maybe you should make time," Kelsey suggested, deliberately keeping a smile on her lips.

His expression, as well as his tone, was noncommittal. "I'll think about it."

She wasn't exactly sure why, but Kelsey felt that the reluctant policeman needed a gentle push in the right direction. Turning toward Mike, she asked, "When's the next time the Angels are in town, Mike?"

Mike didn't have to check a schedule. He knew all the home games by heart, no matter what the sport. Home games allowed him to remain here with Miranda instead of traipsing around the country, following the native teams to other stadiums.

"They're home next Friday. They're playing—"

"Doesn't matter," Kelsey waved away the rest of her brother's words. "Can you get two tickets to that game?"

"Sure."

"You're planning on going, too?" Travis asked, surprised. As far as he knew, his sister wasn't really that into sports.

Kelsey's eyes met Morgan's and her mouth curved. "Yeah. I thought it might be fun."

As attractive as Kelsey Marlowe was, Morgan didn't want to get sucked into going anywhere with her. Maybe *because* she was so attractive, he speculated. No sense in inviting trouble to pull up a chair at his table.

He shook his head, wondering how many ways he could refuse an offer before they thought of him as rude. "No point in getting the tickets. I might still be working on the car," he pointed out.

"Glad you brought that up," Bryan said, putting down his fork. "I won't hear of you working on my wife's car without getting paid for your trouble."

Morgan's eyes met his. Bryan liked to think of himself as an excellent judge of character. As a lawyer, sometimes he had only a couple of minutes to make up his mind if a person was being truthful or artfully lying. From what he could tell, Donnelly looked like a straight arrow.

"Not doing it for the money," Morgan informed him, telling him the same thing he'd told Kelsey the other day. "I used to do it for extra money after school. Now it's a hobby. I like to keep my hand in."

"I understand that," Bryan told him. "But there's no reason a man can't make money at his hobby. Besides, I'd really feel a lot better about this if you gave me some sort of a reckoning when you finish." Although genially stated, it was clear that there was no arguing with the man's tone.

Kelsey leaned into Morgan and said in a stage whisper, "You'd better do as he says. He's a lawyer and he'll talk your ear off if you don't give in. My dad knows at least twenty different ways to approach any problem. Sometimes more."

"Twenty-five," Bryan corrected with an enigmatic smile that was just mysterious enough to elude being pinned down. Morgan had no idea if the man was kidding or not.

But he knew enough not to argue at his hosts' table. "Fine. I'll work up some sort of bill when I'm finished." Although he'd already decided to pass the cost of the parts on, he'd intended to throw in the labor for free. Morgan made the promise to give Bryan a bill predominantly to end the discussion.

Intuitively sensing what was on Morgan's mind, Kelsey thought it only fair to warn the policeman. "My Dad'll hold you to that, you know. He only *looks* easygoing."

Morgan nodded. "Thanks for the heads-up."

"I couldn't help but notice the accent," Trent commented. "How long have you been in California?"

"A little more than two and a half years," Morgan answered.

"What brought you here? Other than the weather, I mean," Trevor asked. He ran a restaurant that saw a good deal of traffic, both native and tourist, and people and what motivated them interested him perhaps almost as much as sports did Mike.

"My car," Morgan replied.

The answer drew a laugh and drained away some of the residual tension still hovering around the room. The response was, Morgan thought, the better choice. Initially he was going to say he came here because it was as far away from "there" as he could go in the continental United States. But that would only give rise to more questions. Questions he didn't want to answer.

Conversation at the table continued in a more relaxed vein. Perforce dinner lasted longer than Morgan was accustomed to. Ordinarily, dinner was something he ate in snatches while doing something else—sitting on a stakeout, working on a car or watching something on TV. Dinner was not something that required his sitting down formally at a table and concentrating on what he was consuming.

But he had to admit, his guard slipping just a fraction of an inch, he found sharing the meal with the Marlowes different and maybe, just maybe, somewhat enjoyable, as well.

When it was over and Morgan rose to his feet, offering to clear the table and "take care of the dishes," Kate merely patted his hand and told him not to worry about it.

"You're a guest here, Morgan. That means no work.

Besides, I have sons, daughters-in-law, a future daughter-in-law," she nodded at Shana, "and a dishwasher to handle what you see here. None of them would mind helping me, right?" Her bright, animated eyes swept over the other occupants at the table.

"What about Kelsey?" Travis wanted to know. "Why isn't she included in this 'willing' group?"

"Kelsey came to the hospital, so she's off the hook," Kate said serenely.

"We would have come to the hospital if we'd known," Trevor protested. It was obvious that he wanted her to know that. To remember that each one of them loved her dearly and that she was important to them.

"Water under the bridge, boys," Kelsey said cheerfully.

"I can think of something else that, with very little effort, could be in the water under the bridge," Mike commented, eyeing Kelsey pointedly.

"Don't threaten your sister with a policeman here, Mike," Bryan said, doing his best to sound serious. "She disappears, he'll remember."

"Kelsey, why don't you take Morgan into the living room?" Kate suggested.

Shana, Venus and Miranda were already stacking the dinner plates while Laurel was busy cleaning up the minute crumbs that encircled Cody's plate. Miranda nudged Mike, indicating that the effort was not restricted to a single gender.

"Perhaps offer him a drink?" Kate added, looking at her daughter.

"If he has to put up with Kelsey on a one-on-one

basis, he's going to need more than one," Travis told his mother, joining his fiancée. He looked at Morgan. "The liquor cabinet is over on the left as you walk in."

"I'm sorry about that," Kelsey apologized as they went into the living room.

Morgan assumed that she was referring to the conversation at the table. It had gone on for a while. Somewhat amused, he asked, "Which part?"

She watched him for a long moment. "I was referring to when Cody asked you if you really had no one."

Morgan merely shrugged. "He's just a little boy. He doesn't know better."

Well, that was forgiving of him. He'd surprised her. He didn't seem the type to differentiate between children and adults.

"I'm also sorry that you don't have anyone," she added in a lower voice.

Again he shrugged, but this time he glanced away. The lack of eye contact bothered her. "It happens."

His tone was dismissive, but her gut told her that he was withholding something. "How did it happen to you?"

"Isn't this what you were just apologizing for?"

"I apologized because Cody said what he did out in the open. This is in private." She nodded, indicating the room. "Between you and me."

Their eyes met. "What if I don't want something private between you and me?"

A lesser person would have flinched, if not backed down altogether. But she had grown up in a love-torment relationship with her brothers and it had hardened her a great deal. Kelsey returned his gaze, never wavering for a moment.

The tension was back. But it was a different kind of tension that crackled and sizzled between them. It made her acutely aware of just how close he was standing.

She took a breath. "Don't you?" she asked in a quiet voice.

Damn, where had this sudden need come from? He neither expected it nor welcomed it. He certainly didn't want it. Simply being aware of it was disconcerting enough.

"You don't want to get mixed up with me, Kelsey," he warned her.

Kelsey knew a challenge when she heard one.

Oh God, she loved a challenge. Just hearing Morgan say the words heightened the warm, fluid desire suddenly and capriciously flowing through her veins.

"Maybe I do and maybe I don't," she said philosophically. "The point is, you don't know me well enough to say that."

"No," he admitted, granting her that, "but I know me well enough to say it."

Had he come right out and said that he was attracted to her, it would have most likely made her step back—although she wasn't a hundred percent sure about that. The fact that he was pushing her away for her "own good" had just the opposite effect. It utterly intrigued her. She'd always wanted what she couldn't have.

"Maybe," she allowed. "But I like making up my own mind, Officer Donnelly."

He knew where this was going. And part of him wanted it to. Still, because he had a conscience, he warned her again. "You're going to regret this."

Not at first. I'd bet my life on that. She could feel her pulse accelerating at the promise of what was to come.

"We'll see," she murmured.

Morgan couldn't really say if he was the one who ultimately made the first move or if Kelsey had. He vaguely believed that it was him, but he couldn't have sworn to it.

Whatever space there had been between them evaporated completely. Within the confines of an erratic heartbeat, his lips were against hers.

He was also aware that for however long the kiss went on, time stood still. The moment was filled with an incredible rush of warmth and a surge of desire, desire that had not been aroused or even so much as nominally nudged for the past two and a half years.

Ever since he'd buried his wife and child, and his heart.

Kelsey's heart slammed into her rib cage with the force of an aimed ground-to-missile rocket. For perhaps the first time in her life, she'd gotten more than she'd bargained for.

Kelsey drew her head back, all but completely overwhelmed by what she'd just experienced. She had to glance down to reassure herself that the ground was still there beneath her feet and that it hadn't been fried to a crisp, the way she'd thought it—and she—had.

"What's your pleasure?" she heard herself ask in a shaky voice. The look on Donnelly's face told her that she needed to elaborate. It took massive control to keep a telltale color from creeping into her cheeks. "To drink," she added with a bit too much emphasis. "What would you like to drink?" As an afterthought, she waved her hand toward the honey-colored liquor cabinet.

"Nothing," he answered. "I don't think I should have anything." He hadn't told her about his father, and now wasn't the time. Instead, he fell back on a typical explanation. "I'm leaving soon and—"

Kelsey stopped him before he could finish. "You leave 'soon' and I'll never hear the end of it."

"I don't understand."

"My brothers'll tease me that I chased you away." Even though they were all grown-up, there was no end to the things her brothers found to tease her about.

Kelsey had a feisty element to her. He'd tasted it in her kiss. Even when she'd leaned into him, there hadn't been a hint of surrender. He had a feeling she was hell on wheels in *any* situation.

"You do that often? Chase guys away?"

She laughed shortly. "Most of the time, my brothers were the ones who chased guys away." And then, because she was highly protective of them just as they were of her, and she didn't want Donnelly getting the wrong impression of her brothers, Kelsey added, "They tend to be overprotective."

"I didn't get that impression."

"That's because they probably think you have the good sense not to want to go out with me."

Damn but this woman was sexy, and just about the

last thing he needed in his life. "Is that what it is—good sense?"

"According to my brothers," she emphasized, her words emerging slowly.

"I seem to recall you offering to go to a ball game with me," he reminded her.

She couldn't take her eyes off him. Things she'd promised herself to avoid melted away. "They don't see that as a date." Her mouth got exceedingly dry. Like cotton in single-digit humidity. "What do you see it as?"

He heard a sigh and abruptly realized that it had come from him.

"Something that's not going to happen," he told her matter-of-factly. "The vice president is arriving in Orange County for a fund-raiser. Every available man and woman in blue is being asked to turn up to make sure that the visit goes smoothly." Otherwise, he thought, there was more than a fifty-fifty chance that he'd wind up proving her brothers wrong, despite his own common sense and logical intentions.

Disappointment skewered her. Kelsey did her best not to show it and even succeeded in sounding somewhat nonchalant. "Why didn't you just say so earlier?"

He shrugged, as if his interest in the subject was barely engaged. "Maybe I was just curious to see how it would play out." His eyes met hers. "I did say I couldn't go," he reminded her.

Was he just jerking her around? Or was there some-thing else at work here? Kelsey was familiar with self-preservation. Was that what he was trying to do? Was he afraid to make a connection?

Welcome to the club, Donnelly, she thought.

Out loud, she said, "Because you said you'd still be working on my mother's car. That meant you were making a personal choice and choosing not to go. A work detail isn't personal."

"So you don't mind being rejected if it's because the VP is coming, but you do mind if I say I can't make it because I'm busy."

For reasons of pride, Kelsey was about to deny his assumption, then thought better of it. Better to keep things simple, she decided.

"Something like that." And then, seeing his reaction, she laughed. "Don't look so concerned, Officer Donnelly. I'm not measuring you for a formal tuxedo and looking at matching rings. I just want to have a little fun at a ball game." *And maybe a little more afterward.* "The last thing in the world I want to do is become emotionally involved with a policeman."

She said the last with a finality that caught his attention.

"Mind if I ask why?"

This time she was the one who shrugged carelessly. Or tried to make it look that way. "Let's just say that I discovered that Newport Beach's 'finest' didn't live up to its name."

"How so?"

"You get to ask questions but I don't?"

"I do this for a living," he replied solemnly. "But you can ask questions, too."

Looking into his eyes, she could see what wasn't being said. "You just don't have to answer them, right?"

His mouth curved. God help him, but he liked her. Liked her spirit. "Right. Neither do you."

She rolled that around in her head for a moment. "Sounds fair," she pronounced. "So you're really working next Friday?"

"Yes, I'm really working next Friday."

"Dodgers are in town the following weekend." She remembered Mike mentioning that. "Anyone need guarding the Friday after next?"

He didn't know what it was about this woman, or why he felt this fire lighting inside of him. He knew this wasn't going to go anywhere. *Couldn't* go anywhere. For a number of reasons. It only made sense to back away right now. Make up some excuse and pull the curtain down.

And yet…

"Need guarding?" he repeated. "I've got a feeling that I might."

The answer delighted her and she laughed. A deep, throaty laugh that he felt go right into the center of his gut, tightening it.

"You don't know the half of it, Officer Donnelly," she said.

That, he realized, was just what he was afraid of. Or should be afraid of if he had half a brain, Morgan corrected. But right now, heaven help him, he was intrigued. And so powerfully drawn to this petite, dynamite stick of a woman that he felt completely tied up in knots inside.

"I've got this strong feeling," he said, just before he gave in to the urge to kiss her again, "that you're going to show me."

Chapter Nine

"Maybe I'd better go," Morgan heard himself saying eons later when he finally forced himself to end the kiss that geometrically grew in intensity with every moment that passed by.

Had they been alone...

But they hadn't been alone and that was a very good thing. Otherwise, mistakes would have been made.

More mistakes, he silently corrected, because this shouldn't have happened, either. Despite the fact that the kiss had rattled him down to his very toes, it had opened a door that should have remained closed if he was to have any peace.

Okay, what was going on here? Kelsey silently demanded. Why did she feel like some schoolgirl who'd just been introduced to her first grown-up kiss? She wasn't exactly a novice at this kind of thing, and the fact that she hadn't been dating recently had been of her own choosing, *not* because no one was asking.

But goodness, she couldn't recall *anyone* ever stirring up her soul like that. No one had ever completely sapped away her breath or made her pulse race in the same way.

Stunned, trying to focus on a world that had suddenly gone utterly out of focus, she nodded in response to Morgan's announcement that he should be leaving.

"You'll call me?" she asked, her voice low and husky. "About my mother's car, you'll call me?" she clarified after a beat, realizing that, left standing alone, her original question sounded as if she wanted him to call her for a date.

"The minute it's done," he promised.

It was difficult to sound distant when his breath kept cutting out on him. He hadn't been close to winded when he chased down a perp last week. So why would he be so breathless from kissing Kelsey?

Morgan cleared his throat. "Tell your mother thanks for dinner. Your father, too," he added as an afterthought. "It was…nice." *Nice* was a paltry word, but right now he didn't trust his voice to say anything lengthier.

"You can tell them yourself," she suggested, gesturing toward the dining room. Judging from the noise, she'd guess that the table was still being cleared away.

But Morgan already had the door open, eager to make his getaway. "Gotta go."

The next second, he was gone.

Amusement curved her mouth as Kelsey stood staring at the closed door. Had she just frightened off the big, strong, strapping policeman? Certainly looked that way.

Makes two of us, Donnelly.

Travis looked in, glancing around the room. "Where's Morgan?"

"Gone," she told him simply, then turned around to face her brother. "He went home."

The news surprised him. "God, Kelsey, what did you do to the man?" Travis asked. He jerked his thumb behind him. "He didn't even come back into the dining room to get his jacket."

"I didn't do anything to him," she informed Travis, breezing passed him. "He kissed me."

"Well, that explains it," Travis commented. "You can be pretty scary when your lips are moving."

She didn't bother answering her brother. Instead, she walked into the dining room.

Morgan's jacket was hanging on the back of the chair just where he'd left it. She made straight for it and went through the pockets.

Watching her, Travis and Trent, the only other occupants in the room at the moment, exchanged looks and grinned.

"Usually you're a little more subtle than that," Trent observed.

Kelsey glanced up for a moment, pulling her lips into a quick smile before continuing with her examination. "No, I'm not. You're just not around that much anymore." And then, so they wouldn't start up about how snoopy she was, she explained, "I'm just making sure Morgan doesn't have anything in his pockets that he might need." She drew out the last word as her fingers came in contact with something she judged Officer Morgan Donnelly needed a great deal.

Withdrawing her hand from the jacket's inside pocket, Kelsey held the prize triumphantly aloft. "He left his wallet."

"He's going to need that," Trent commented.

Kelsey tucked the wallet back into the inside pocket and draped the jacket over her arm. "My thoughts exactly."

Travis put his hand out to her. "I could—" He never got to finish his statement.

Anticipating what he was going to say, Kelsey cut him off. "So could I."

"You know, this isn't like you, Kelse," Trent observed. Travis nodded in agreement.

"What?" she asked innocently. "Being thoughtful?" And then her eyebrows narrowed as she warned, "And, if I were either of you, I'd think very carefully before I answered that."

Travis held up his hands in a symbolic surrender. "Wasn't going to say another word."

"Me neither," Trent chimed in.

Which was how Mike found them as he walked into the room with Miranda. He looked from one sibling to another. "What's this all about?"

Travis was quick to volunteer the information. "Kelsey ran Morgan off so fast, he forgot his jacket and his wallet."

Okay, enough was enough. "I did *not* run the man off," Kelsey protested.

Shifting over to stand beside her sister-in-law, Miranda draped her arm across Kelsey's slender shoulders. "Stop picking on your sister, Mike."

"Me?" Mike cried incredulously. He pointed a finger at the triplet closest to him. "Travis was the one who said she ran Donnelly off."

"Okay, then all three of you," Miranda amended, bringing Trent into it just in case he'd said something before she walked in. "Stop picking on your sister," she said with the kind of feeling reserved for someone who was part of the family.

Kelsey flashed her sister-in-law a grateful, conspiratorial grin. "Thanks, Miranda. Will you tell my mom that I had to run an errand but that I should be back in a little while?"

Miranda turned so that her back was to the male members of the family. She mouthed, "Unless you get lucky" to Kelsey.

"Not looking for that to happen," Kelsey assured her with feeling.

Grabbing her purse from the table by the front door, she was out of the house before anyone could say anything else to her.

Donnelly was going to need this, she told herself, briskly walking down the driveway. She was only being responsible. Although, she could have just as easily called up and left a message on his machine, telling him that he'd forgotten his jacket.

She was fairly certain that Morgan would have realized he'd left his wallet in his jacket pocket without her having to mention it. That way, he wouldn't have known that she'd gone through the pockets.

Reaching her car, she opened the driver's side and tossed his jacket on the passenger seat before getting in. She started the car, then backed it out of the driveway.

Traffic was light. She glanced at the jacket again. As a rule, men didn't like having their pockets—especially their wallets—ransacked.

Because that was where they kept their secrets, she thought, remembering. Her jawline hardened. Had she not absently browsed through Dan's wallet, waiting for him to finish his shower, she would have never found the wedding photograph he kept stuffed between two credit cards.

The pain of that discovery returned to her in spades, twisting her gut.

She recalled looking at the creased photograph for a long time, trying to come up with excuses for its existence. Excuses that explained why he stood beside a woman wearing a wedding gown. Excuses that explained why, if that woman was either his ex-wife or his late wife, he hadn't gotten around to mentioning that little fact. Even *after* he'd started talking about marriage.

The moment Dan had come out of the bathroom, a towel loosely wrapped around his hips and water still clinging to his hair, and seen her holding the photograph, he'd stumbled over his tongue. She'd never seen him so flustered.

A man who had nothing to hide, who wasn't guilty of abusing her heart, wouldn't have stumbled over his own tongue, wouldn't have alternated between anger and repentance, she thought.

God, but she'd been such a trusting idiot, Kelsey upbraided herself.

Amid a barrage of angry words, she'd thrown Dan out and then called Travis, asking him to have his firm's investigator find out all he could about Dan.

It didn't take long. All her worse fears were proved correct. He was married. With a baby on the way. Dan had still tried to explain his way out of it, but she refused to listen. Instead, she warned him that if he ever came near her again, she would call his wife and tell her everything.

She never saw Dan again.

Remembering that, remembering how she'd felt, knowing she'd been duped, Kelsey suddenly pulled over to the side of the road. Putting the car into Park and pulling up the emergency brake, she let the car idle as she took the wallet out of Morgan's pocket.

The mental tug-of-war went on for less than a minute. She needed to know she wasn't setting herself up again. Needed to know that Donnelly was exactly what he seemed, a single man.

There wasn't much in his wallet beyond his license, his police ID, his insurance card and a few bills in a separate compartment that added up to thirty-three dollars.

The last place she checked was inside the fold intended for credit cards. That was when she found it. A single incriminating photograph. The kind of professional photograph taken in a studio. Her heart hurt as she stared at the photograph of Morgan standing beside a slender woman with long, blond hair. In his arms he was holding a little towheaded girl between them. She looked to be younger than two years old.

In a hazy, bizarre way, Kelsey was aware of cars whizzing by.

Damn it. Kelsey closed her eyes. They stung. Donnelly wasn't worth the tears that seeped out between her lashes, she thought angrily.

"When are you going to learn?" she demanded angrily, her voice a hoarse whisper. "When the hell are you ever going to learn?"

Furious with herself, with Morgan, Kelsey started the car again. She almost plowed into an SUV, slamming on her brakes at the last second and pulling back onto the shoulder of the road. Her heart pounding, she watched through tears to make sure that there was no other vehicle about to barrel into her before she pulled back onto the road.

The bastard!

The lousy bastard. Acting so reserved, so damn polite when all the time…

Kelsey pushed down on the accelerator. For once, she drove without checking her rearview mirror every few minutes to make sure there was no police car behind her. She was far too angry for that.

She got to Morgan's single-story house in record time. Leaving her car parked askew in his driveway, she had to double back to shut her door. She'd left it hanging open.

Her anger building with each passing second, Kelsey strode up to Morgan's front door and rang the bell. When there was no instant reply, she started knocking, then pounding on his door with her fist.

"Damn it, Donnelly, I know you're in there. Open the damn door!"

The door opened just as she was about to pound on it again. He appeared puzzled and more than a little surprised to see her.

Guilty and worried, most likely, Kelsey thought hotly. His wife was probably around somewhere and he would have to explain what she was doing here if he couldn't get rid of her.

Good. He deserved to be skewered, she thought angrily.

Kelsey threw his jacket at him. "You forgot your jacket," she snapped, pushing her way past him and striding into the living room.

"Thanks." He glanced down at the crumpled jacket. Until this moment, he hadn't realized he'd left it. Kissing Kelsey had played havoc with his mind. But at least he wasn't playing Dr. Jekyll and Mr. Hyde at the same time, like Kelsey was. "Are you all right?" he asked, closing the door again.

"I'm just ginger peachy," Kelsey ground out.

He assumed that her anger was somehow connected to her bringing the jacket over. "You could have just called and I would have come back for the jacket. You didn't have to go out of your way to drop it off."

Instead of calming her, his words had the exact opposite effect. "You would have preferred that, wouldn't you? That way, you could be sure that I wouldn't run into her." Kelsey strode around the room, glancing toward the hall as she raised her voice so that it would carry to other parts of the house. "Been lucky so far, but luck only hangs on so long, right?"

He draped his jacket over the arm of the sofa, staring at Kelsey. "What are you talking about?"

She swung around to glare at him, her hands fisted at her waist. "Don't play dumb. I'm talking about your wife."

He didn't answer for a moment. Everything inside of him went eerily silent and dark. And then he asked, his voice hardly louder than a whisper, "What?"

Oh, no, she wasn't buying into that dumb act. She was through being a trusting idiot. To think she actually had been entertaining the idea of sleeping with him. God, but she was hopeless.

"You have a picture of your wife and daughter in your wallet." She threw the accusation at him. "Don't bother denying it."

"That I've got a picture of them? Why should I?"

"No, that you've *got* a wife and daughter."

His eyes narrowed as the first part of what she'd said suddenly replayed itself in his head. "You went through my wallet." His voice was flat.

"No, I'm clairvoyant," she retorted flippantly. "How else would I know about them? Of course I went through your wallet."

"Why?" The single word shimmered between them, lethal. Loaded.

Throwing up her hands, Kelsey began to pace around the room, something she did when she was very angry or very agitated. Right now, she was both.

"Because, like an idiot, I was hoping I wouldn't find anything. But I did." *And it broke my heart.* "I thought you were different, but you're just like the rest of them," she accused.

He was doing his best to control his temper and understand. "'Them?'"

Was he *trying* to play dumb, or was he just dense? "Yes, *them.* Men. Policemen," she amended because none of her brothers or her father belonged to this hateful brotherhood of lecherous creatures who blissfully lied their way into a woman's bed. She stopped pacing and hurdled another accusation at him. "You *kissed* me."

How could he have done that? How could he have kissed her while he was married to such a beautiful, trusting woman? She could literally see the love, the trust in the woman's eyes.

To rein in his anger, Morgan started to grow distant. "I rather thought it was mutual. We kissed each other."

"Okay, maybe," she granted. "Only difference is, I'm not married."

This tirade of hers finally made sense. "You think I'm married?"

"Aren't you?" The second she said it, Kelsey secretly prayed that Morgan could convince her that he was single. That the woman in the photograph was a relative. A sister maybe. Even an ex-wife. Anyone but his present wife.

If he wanted this strange connection to end, all he had to do was tell her yes, he was married. Yes, that woman in the photograph was his wife, Beth, and the little girl he was holding was his daughter, Amy. Once that was established, Kelsey Marlowe would curse him and stomp out of his life, leaving it just as empty as it had been before she'd come on the scene.

So why wasn't he telling her that? Why wasn't he gratefully grabbing at the excuse Kelsey and fate had just presented him on a silver platter? It was the only sensible course of action. Telling her made sense in so many ways. And yet, here he stood, mutely watching her all but burn up like a meteor barreling into the earth's atmosphere. Why?

The answer was painfully obvious. Because he wanted her, wanted Kelsey, far-reaching complications and all.

"Well?" she finally demanded, breaking the silence. "Don't you have anything to say? Are you or aren't you married?" Her hands were back on her hips. She stood a scant few inches away from Morgan, pugnaciously challenging him. "Lie to me. I dare you."

"If I was going to lie to you," Morgan finally said, his voice dangerously low. "I'd tell you that I was married."

It took her a second to digest that. "Then you're not married?"

"No."

Damn it, she knew how easy it was for someone to

lie to her. Why was there this sudden burst of hope exploding in her chest, radiating out to all corners of her?

Stay on point, Kelsey. You don't want to be taken for another ride. Not again.

She didn't want to walk away from him, either. What did that make her?

The answer was easy. Crazy.

She needed a push in the right direction, Kelsey reminded herself fiercely. "That isn't your wife in the photograph?"

He looked down at it again. It still hurt to see Beth and Amy. Hurt because they were no longer in his life. Was it always going to be that way? Would he ever be numbed to the pain?

"I didn't say that."

What was he trying to do, confuse her with fancy footwork and rhetoric? "So she *is* your wife," Kelsey pressed.

Morgan paused for a long moment, as he waited for the pain in his gut to subside. "You have your tenses wrong," he finally told her.

Chapter Ten

"My tenses?" Kelsey repeated, confused. "What are you talking about?"

Now that he had opened the door, he couldn't very well shut it in her face, even though talking about this hurt like hell.

"Beth *was* my wife."

"You're divorced?"

The moment stretched out between them until she could almost swear she heard it creaking. And then he finally said, "No."

The moment the word was out, she understood. Understood and felt horribly guilty, ashamed and a whole host of other emotions that all but stampeded right over her. He meant that his wife was dead. And she had stirred that up for him.

"And your daughter?" she asked hoarsely. She'd come this far, she had to know.

This time, Morgan didn't answer. He just looked at her and she saw it, saw the anguish that was in his soul reflected in his eyes.

"Oh God," she whispered, her heart aching for him. "How?"

His voice was flat, emotionless and all the more frightening for it. "Does it matter?"

"No," she answered quietly. Telling him that she asked because she felt for him, wanted to share his pain, to make it an iota lighter, didn't seem appropriate right now. He wouldn't believe her anyway. "I am so sorry, Morgan. I didn't mean to hurt you by bringing it up. I was just…"

His eyes darkened. "Just what?"

The whisper sent chills down her spine. They weren't the kind of chills she would have welcomed. "I was just afraid."

"Afraid of what?"

Back away. Make something up. Just get out of there, she ordered herself.

But instead of saying something vague and shrugging him off, Kelsey heard herself telling him the truth. "Of being sucked in again. Of being made a fool of."

Kelsey dragged her hand through her hair and blew out a none-too-steady breath. She didn't talk about this, ever, not to her brothers, not even to her mother who knew everything else about her. But she owed Morgan a measure of penance for stirring up memories he clearly would have preferred leaving undisturbed and for storming in on him in the first place.

Wanting to pace, she forced herself to remain still. "I was—for lack of a better word—involved with a policeman a little over a year ago. He was handsome, charming and so wonderful I kept wanting to pinch myself because I couldn't believe he was real."

"Let me guess—he wasn't."

"My story, let me tell it my way," Kelsey instructed, struggling to keep her voice matter-of-fact. It wasn't easy. She pressed her lips together, then continued. "I wound up falling in love with him. He even talked about marrying me."

She was laying herself bare. The hurt in her voice burrowed into his indifference. "So what happened? Your brothers run him off?"

Kelsey laughed shortly. "My brothers would have killed him if they'd found out."

"That he was sleeping with you?"

She gave a half shrug. "That would have gotten them perturbed. What would have ticked them off was finding out that Dan was married." Kelsey didn't want to continue explaining. She looked at Morgan, praying he would connect the dots and understand. That he would forgive her over-the-top reaction. "So when I saw that photograph in your wallet—"

"You jumped to conclusions," Donnelly finished for her.

From where she stood, it sounded like a harsh accusation. But she knew she deserved it. She had no business invading his privacy, no real business going through his wallet.

Kelsey nodded. "I have a tendency of doing that. I'm sorry." Kelsey rounded out her apology. "I shouldn't have gone through your wallet. I shouldn't have carried on like that. And I wouldn't have if I didn't—"

She stopped abruptly. Too much, she was giving away too much. He had enough for a valid apology. She'd ripped out her heart, she didn't have to barbecue it. Exhaling slowly, she vainly sought some source of inner calm.

But that still eluded her. "If you have no objections, Officer Donnelly, I really would like to start over."

He looked like an immobile statue as he said, "I wouldn't."

"Oh." Okay, what did she do with that? she wondered, a sinking feeling in her stomach taking hold. She needed some kind of graceful exit line.

Nothing came to mind.

"Mistakes are to learn from," he told her. "With any luck, they wind up making you a better person."

Morgan paused again, wrestling with words he knew were going to hurt if he said them. But she had put herself out there to make amends. He could do no less.

"I lost Beth and Amy two and a half years ago to a drunk driver. That was just after my father had killed himself. With my service revolver."

"Oh God."

He continued as if he hadn't heard her. He laughed shortly, shaking his head. "It seems oddly ironic that everything bad in my life involved alcohol somehow. My father used to drink because he couldn't handle life without my mother. Drank himself right into a stroke. He didn't die, although he wanted to, but he was paralyzed from the waist down. That made him feel like half a man. Eventually, the half that still functioned killed the half that didn't." He closed his eyes for a moment. "There was an inquiry—"

She didn't understand. "An inquiry? By whom? Into what?"

"By the police. Into me."

Morgan saw indignation enter her eyes and thought it almost amusing. And strangely touching. She knew next to nothing about him and yet she was indignant for him, taking offense that this had happened to him. Why?

"My father shot himself. The coroner thought it might have been a mercy killing." He saw the question Kelsey wasn't asking. "It wasn't," he said firmly, then relented. "At least, not consciously."

"I don't understand."

"Before I became a policeman, I used to go to the gun range to practice shooting. I wanted to become a letter-perfect marksman." Morgan shoved his hands into his pockets. "When I got married and moved out, I left my old gun in the house. I don't know why," he said honestly and then shrugged. "Maybe I wanted to help relieve his suffering without having him on my conscience, I don't know."

"You're not like that."

She sounded so convinced, so sure. "How would

you know?" he asked, controlled anger rippling through his voice. "A few minutes ago, you thought I was capable of it."

"No, I didn't," she told him. "I just wanted to hear you say you didn't do it."

It still made no sense to him. People just weren't unconditionally trusting like that. "How would you know I wasn't lying to you?"

She couldn't say why she suddenly knew that he wouldn't lie to her, she just did. She was so certain of it that she would have been willing to bet everything she had that he was telling her the truth. For some reason she couldn't put into words, in these last few minutes, something in her soul had connected with his.

She really felt bad about the accusations she'd hurled at him.

Kelsey doubted if Morgan would understand if she told him what she was feeling. She wasn't completely sure she understood it herself. But it didn't change the fact that she *knew* he was being truthful.

She smiled at him, her heart both aching for Morgan and filling with empathy.

Empathy and maybe something more.

Morgan was a wounded soul, and in a way that was minor when compared to what he'd gone through, so was she.

Morgan was still waiting for her to answer. "Let's just say I've had an epiphany and it made me realize that you couldn't have done something like that," she told him simply.

He scratched his head. The woman blew hot and then cold—and confused the hell out of him. "You're one hell of a strange person, Kelsey Marlowe."

The grin on her lips reached her eyes, lighting them up. "My brothers would tend to agree with you." It was time to go. Before she found a way to put her other foot into her mouth. "Well, I brought you your jacket and wallet—"

A hint of amusement curved his mouth. "Not to mention a barrage of accusations."

She nodded self-consciously. "That, too," she allowed. Kelsey glanced toward the front door. "I'd better be going."

Now that things were no longer adversarial, he relaxed a little. And realized that he didn't want her to leave just yet. Having her here pushed the loneliness back. "You can stay for a while if you like."

Their eyes held for a moment. "I'd like that very much."

Her tone was silken and he realized something more. If they stayed inside the house, things might get complicated. He couldn't uninvite her without looking like an idiot. And then a way out occurred to him. "How are you at taking orders?"

Where had that come from? "Excuse me?"

He nodded toward the side of the house that led into the garage. "I could use some help working on your mother's car. Since you're here, I thought you might want to lend a hand."

She hadn't expected that. But from the little bit she'd picked up last night, she found she rather liked watching a car being taken apart and fixed. The prospect intrigued her. "Sure. Fine. Just lead the way."

He started to, then stopped for a moment as he asked, "What do you know about cars?"

"More than I did before I came over last night," she answered brightly.

Morgan sighed. "I guess I've got my work cut out for me."

Kelsey offered no argument, only a smile. "I guess so."

Morgan rested the torque wrench on the padded towel he had draped on the left side of the opened hood. They'd been at this for two hours now. "You follow orders better than I thought you would."

Despite the cool evening, Kelsey had managed to work up a sweat. Brushing the perspiration off from her forehead with the back of her hand, she grinned. She had a feeling Morgan did not dispense praise freely. "Glad I could surprise you."

It was getting late. "We've done a fair share of work," he told her. Putting the wrench back where it belonged on the wall, he crossed back to the car and dropped the hood back down. "But that's enough for one night." Turning away from the car, he looked at her. "Hold still."

"Why?" Had she done something wrong? Was she about to step on something crawling around on the floor? The thought made her heart jump. Black widows had a tendency to seek out warmth in the corners of garages and under rocks. She hated black widow spiders.

"You've got some grease on your forehead." Using

the edge of his handkerchief, he wiped the smudge away. And as he did, Morgan realized that flicker of attraction was alive and well—and getting stronger. He dropped his hand to his side. "You'd better get going," he urged.

Rather than settle down, her heart was still jumping around. A great deal.

"Do you want me to?" she heard herself asking, her voice barely above a whisper.

"No," he told her honestly, his eyes never leaving hers. "Which is why you should go." *Otherwise, things could go in a whole new direction. And they really shouldn't.*

Her breath grew short. There was hardly enough air in her lungs for her to say, "Funny, it sounds more like a reason to stay to me."

"Neither one of us wants this to go anywhere," Morgan told her quietly. Even though he believed what he was saying, his words sounded as if they lacked conviction, even to him.

"Speak for yourself, Officer Donnelly."

Taking the rag that he'd picked up out of his hands, Kelsey let it drop onto the hood as she rose up on her toes.

The words she'd uttered slipped along his skin, warming his face. Heating his blood. Morgan could feel his gut tightening.

And his desire growing.

"I thought I was speaking for you," he said, each word making its appearance slowly, in a measured cadence that seemed to take a great deal of effort just to push out.

Kelsey moved her head slowly from side to side,

her eyes never leaving his. "Nope," she murmured. "You weren't."

"If I kiss you again," he warned even as he wove his arms around her, drawing her closer, "I'm not going to stop there."

He saw the hint of a smile in her eyes. Saw the same smile curving her mouth. "Promises, promises," she murmured.

There was a sense of danger here that he didn't encounter on the street. On the street, he knew the odds, knew the chances he was taking. This was walking a high wire without a net. One misstep and it was all over. "I'm not kidding, Kelsey."

She could feel her heart racing. Felt excitement starting to build. Her voice was husky with anticipation as she said, "I certainly hope not."

Kelsey's lips were only inches from his. So close he could all but taste them against his own. Taste every word as it was spoken.

His body throbbed.

How much was a man supposed to take? How long could he resist something he wanted so badly? Something, even as he wanted it, he knew he shouldn't indulge in.

If he was sensible, he would just walk away.

But he wasn't sensible. And he couldn't walk away.

"Whatever happens here is on your head," he told her in one last-ditch effort to scare her off.

The last-ditch effort failed.

He knew it would.

"I know. I accept full responsibility," she whispered. This time, as she spoke, her lips lightly grazed his.

The dam burst. The last straw broke. His mouth came down on hers as his arms tightened around her. He was swept away by his feelings, by his all but overwhelming need for her. A need that seemed to be mushrooming within him even as he tried to assuage it.

But it was impossible.

Morgan had known in his heart that kissing her wasn't going to solve anything, wasn't going to end anything. On the contrary, it sent him launching headfirst into a completely different world. One of their creation. One that only the two of them inhabited.

They might as well have been the last two people on earth.

In her bruised and damaged heart, Kelsey knew Morgan was right. She should have just stopped it while she still had the power to do so. He wouldn't have pushed, wouldn't have insisted. She instinctively knew that wasn't the kind of man he was. Maybe that was why she hadn't allowed him to back away. Hadn't wanted him to back away. Because he would have if she'd asked him.

She wanted a man who cared enough about her, not himself, to take her feelings into account. He was that man.

Besides, his story had gotten to her, had made her open up her heart and bleed for him. And now she was vulnerable. So vulnerable that when intense desires sprang up within her, they all had his name indelibly tattooed on them.

He couldn't stop.

Didn't want to stop.

Knew he should do the right thing and back away, but he just didn't have the strength, the willpower, to do so. It just wasn't in him. If she'd given him a sign, just one little sign that she realized this was a mistake, that she wanted him to pull back, he would have forced himself to stop. For her.

But faced with her compliance, with her fervor and enthusiasm, he couldn't. Couldn't do it alone. Not when her mouth tasted sweeter than any fruit he'd ever had. Not when her skin smelled of vanilla and the scent of her hair made his head swirl.

Holding her fast to him with one arm, he felt around on the wall until he located the switch that would automatically close the garage door, locking them away from prying eyes. He hit the switch and he heard the mechanism slowly begin to grind, sending the door back down into place. It vaguely registered. His mind was otherwise occupied. As were his hands.

God, but she felt soft. Soft and pliable. Touching her was like sifting a small piece of heaven through his fingers.

The fire within him flared. If he wasn't careful, he would wind up ripping off her clothes and taking her right here. Snatching up the last of his control, Morgan picked her up in his arms and pushed open the door that led from the garage into his house.

He felt as if he was stumbling through the dark. His lips never left hers as he made his way in. She was the source of his madness and, for now, the source of his fragile solace, as well.

Once inside the house, Morgan got no farther than the family room.

His passions running rampant in his veins, Morgan was only vaguely aware of undressing Kelsey. He tried to strip away barriers, tossing them aside to get ever closer to the warmth, the heat that he suddenly needed more than he needed to breathe.

The kisses grew deeper, the pace faster.

Morgan felt her fingers, flying along his chest and he realized that she was breathlessly doing to him what he was doing to her. Tearing away anything that got in the way.

Material went flying, replaced by palms that were spread out, pressing hard into warm, willing flesh, replaced by lips eager to sample new tastes and to anoint new regions.

Thoughts came in disjointed pieces and feelings rode on lightning bolts, crackling as they made contact on planes no one else could see or feel.

But they did. They saw, they felt. And most of all, they made love.

Chapter Eleven

He made her want to do insane things, like just be there and absorb what was happening. Savor it and revel in it before disintegrating into hot, spent ashes.

But by nature, Kelsey had never been a passive soul willing to merely accept, to quietly receive. Something inside of her, the competitive streak of being the youngest and only girl in her family, burst forward. She was determined to make Morgan feel as weak in the knees, as ecstatically overwhelmed as she was.

But if this were an actual contest, Kelsey knew she would have come in second. In her own defense, it was hard to concentrate when her insides turned to liquid flame. When the feel of Morgan's lips, his hands, his tongue, his very breath along her skin drove her to a world where coherent thoughts no longer existed. Where only incredible pleasure mattered. And the pursuit of more was the single reason for drawing breath.

She wasn't a novice at lovemaking, but she might as well have been because she had never felt a connection like this before. Never felt as if she were having an out-of-body experience before. Never hit the heights exclusively and more than once before she finally became one with her lover.

She did this time.

Not once, but twice, and then again. Three times she reached a climactic peak. The experience was so fulfilling, she didn't think that there was anything left within her to offer Morgan when, finally, he slid his body along hers.

Balancing his weight on his elbows, he framed her face with his hands a second before he entered her. The moment he did, the dance, wickedly delicious, began, building an impossibly beautiful castle in the sky that kept on rising.

Kelsey tightened her arms around him. She held on as tightly as she could, as if she was afraid that he would let her go and she would wind up freefalling through space.

As the furor built, Kelsey moaned against his lips. Morgan could almost feel the sound pushing the fire in his veins a notch higher. The excitement he felt was barely controllable, barely containable. Although he logically knew it was impossible, she still made him wish this moment could go on forever or at least indefinitely.

But he couldn't hold back any longer.

He needed, *wanted* to scale that ultimate height and

bring her with him. It was a matter of timing and he was good at that, or had been, back when it mattered. Back when he'd been part of the human race and had a wife and child to complete him.

The moment the summit was reached, Morgan could feel the sadness encroaching. Sadness and a feeling of disloyalty because, unlike the handful of other times when he'd had sex with what amounted to a total stranger, doing this with Kelsey somehow mattered. And in mattering, it tarnished the memory of his past life. The sharp blades of guilt were not far behind.

She could feel it.

She could feel Morgan withdrawing from her, not physically, but emotionally. Feel it as if it were a sudden, cold draft that intruded between them, dividing them and wrapping them each in separate, icy sheets.

"I'm sorry," she heard him say. The words instantly froze her heart. "I'm sorry, I shouldn't have done that to you."

She clutched her anger to her. It was all she had. Anger was her weapon, her shield.

Kelsey raised herself up on her elbow so she could look down at his face.

"First of all," she said in a voice she struggled to keep level, "you didn't do it *to* me, you did it *with* me. In case you didn't notice, this wasn't some back-alley assault. You didn't just drag me by the hair behind some Dumpster and 'have your way with me' while I whimpered and pleaded for you to stop." Her eyes flashed angrily. "What we just engaged in was mutual." And she really, really didn't want to regret it, but he was now pushing all the wrong buttons, casting a pall over what had, only moments ago, been glorious.

"And second?" he asked quietly.

Kelsey stared at him as if the man had suddenly lapsed into some foreign tongue. Or had lost his mind. "Excuse me?"

"You said 'first of all.' That would necessarily mean that that there's a 'second of all' on your list. What is it?" he asked.

She raised her chin slightly. Stubbornly. Had her brothers been there, one of them would have warned Morgan that he had just unwittingly stumbled into uncharted territory.

"And second of all," she continued tersely, "who was here with us?"

It was his turn to be confused. Looking at Kelsey, he waited. When she didn't elaborate, he had to ask, "What?"

"Who was here with us?" Kelsey repeated slowly, deliberately. Then, before Morgan could protest that he didn't know what she was talking about, she pressed the point. "While we were making love, there was somebody here with us," she insisted. "Not at first, but definitely now. And whoever it is is making you feel guilty for making love with me." Her eyes never left his. "Is it your wife?"

She got it on the first guess, Morgan thought, irritated with her and with himself for different reasons. He sat up, dragging a hand through his unruly hair. This was all wrong. Damn it, he wouldn't have thought of himself being this weak. "Look, maybe you'd better go home…"

She didn't want it to end this way. Not after she'd scaled such wonderful heights. Because if it did, if she left now, all she would remember would be the argument. And the sharp, painful feeling of being abandoned.

Not only that, but his flatly stated suggestion felt like a slap in the face. She wouldn't stand for being "dismissed." If she left, it would be because she wanted to, not because he told her to.

"I'm not an expert on these things," she said, her voice as flat as his, "and I didn't know your wife, but from what I've picked up, she wouldn't have wanted you to be unhappy. She would have wanted you to move on with your life."

"You're right," he said. She stared into his face and instantly knew that his agreement wasn't a cause for celebration. And she was right. "You didn't know my wife," he continued, his voice sounding as if his throat was tight. "So you can't pretend to know what she would or wouldn't have wanted."

Pulling her clothes to her, Kelsey rose to her feet with the dignity of a princess. "Anyone who loves someone wants only the best for them," she told him stiffly.

The vulnerable, exposed feeling permeating through her went far beyond the fact that she was naked. Kelsey quickly left the room—and him. She made her way toward the rear of the house, hoping to find either the bathroom or a guestroom so that she could hurry into her clothes in isolation. The sooner she was dressed, the sooner she could work on shedding this embarrassed feeling.

Kelsey found a bathroom first.

Shutting the door, she got dressed at lightning speed. If she kept moving quickly, concentrating only on what she was doing, she wouldn't have time to think, to reflect on the glaring fact that she needed to have her head examined.

But why? a small voice inside her pressed. *You're not the one with a problem, Donnelly is. He loved his wife so much, he's completely turned inside out. This isn't about you, Kelse, it's about him. About the pain he's feeling.*

She was her mother's daughter. By the time she was finished getting dressed, her embarrassment—and her anger at being made to feel that way—had vanished. It was replaced by genuine concern for the man she'd left in the other room.

Coming back out, she found Morgan waiting for her, wearing a pair of jeans and nothing else. She hadn't been in a position to fully appreciate it earlier, but the man had a washboard stomach the likes of which made her own stomach quiver. She was surprised some woman hadn't thrown a net over him and dragged him off to her lair way before now.

He appeared uncomfortable. "I didn't mean to insult you," he apologized.

"You didn't." All right, it was a lie, she thought, but his apology had smoothed things out. It also made her want to reach out to him. "Would you like to talk about it?" she coaxed.

"It?" he repeated. Was she referring to their lovemaking? She hadn't struck him as one of those women who constantly needed and wanted to talk about feelings, wanted to explore every moment and its significance ad nauseum. Had he been wrong about her?

She was willing to leave it in vague terms, letting him be the one who elaborated. But nothing that had to do with Donnelly was easy. "Your guilt at being alive when your wife and daughter aren't."

He wasn't about to be psychoanalyzed. "I don't feel guilty."

Kelsey didn't back off. "Don't you?"

He shouldn't have apologized. It had given her a whole new head of steam. "I've got an early morning," he told her, cutting her short.

"So do I." As she spoke, Kelsey made her way to the front door, picking up her purse where she'd dropped it when they came in. "Give me a call when you finish up the car."

The car. He'd forgotten all about that. For a while there, he'd forgotten about everything. Except her. "Yeah."

They left it at that, the single word hanging in the air between them long after she went out the door.

Morgan couldn't get moving, couldn't shake the feeling that he'd behaved like a jerk. Both in allowing himself to get carried away with Kelsey and then in saying what he had to her.

Behaving like that just proved his basic belief: that he had no business getting involved with anyone socially outside the job. He was better off keeping to himself. He'd had happiness with Beth for a short time in his life, but that was over now. If he thought that lightning could strike the same heart twice, well, even that didn't mean that he was a candidate. Until he'd married Beth, he hadn't even thought it could happen once. That it had was a miracle. Guys like him weren't candidates for miracles on any sort of a recurring basis.

Despite her smart mouth, Kelsey Marlowe was a nice girl. He didn't want to mess with her life—any more than he already had, he amended silently.

The cushions on his sofa smelled like jasmine. Jasmine mixed with vanilla. He'd come into the house, exhausted after the double shift he'd been forced to pull. It was the second one in three days. Robbins and Daniels had called in sick—there was a bug going around—and the lieutenant had asked him if he could fill in for one of them. With nothing and no one waiting for him at home, he'd agreed.

But now he was drained. Really drained.

Dropping down onto the sofa, Morgan had instantly detected the scent. It made him think of Kelsey. And just like that, he wasn't drained any longer. He was wired.

He thought of the car still sitting in his garage. None of this would have been going on if he'd just let Kelsey take it to a professional mechanic. It wasn't like him to volunteer to do something without thinking it through first, without weighing any and all possible consequences.

He'd know better next time, he silently promised himself.

Because he felt so wired, Morgan decided to try to

erode his sudden surge of restlessness by working on the car. It was close to being finished. He just needed to paint the fender he'd picked up at a salvage yard. The fit was damn near perfect.

Perfect. Not a word he encountered often, he thought, stopping at his refrigerator to take out a can of beer. But he did have that one night with Kelsey, he remembered, letting the memory drift through his mind in full, animated color.

The next second, annoyed with his lack of control, he dismissed all of it, especially Kelsey. No point in seeing the woman again and further messing up her life. He wasn't exactly a prize worth having in his present state.

And Morgan was fairly confident that he'd never *be* in any other state.

The phone rang just as he was about to go into the garage. He considered ignoring it, then decided that he should pick it up. No one called him at home if it wasn't about work. More than likely, this was the lieutenant, wanting him to come back in for some reason.

Picking up the receiver, he barked, "Donnelly" into the phone. When there was no immediate response, he started to hang up, then tried again just in case it was the lieutenant calling on his cell. Occasional interference in the area tended to block out the clarity of the signal.

"Hello?"

Instead of a deep male voice, he heard a bright female voice say, "Hi." He knew it was her instantly, even before she identified herself. "It's Kelsey. I'm just calling to find out how the car's coming along."

Morgan did his best to ignore the fact that his stomach felt as if it had just encountered a tourniquet and was being squeezed.

"The car's fine." He realized he'd just given human properties to an inanimate object and given her no information on top of that. "It's almost finished," he added.

"And you?"

"I'm not almost finished," he replied tersely.

"No," she said patiently, "I'm asking if you're fine, too." When he didn't answer, she phrased it another way. "Are you okay?"

Ordinarily, he would automatically respond in the affirmative, even if the exact opposite was true. He wasn't into "sharing." And yet, he heard himself saying, "Depends on your definition of 'okay.'"

"The opposite of going to hell on a toboggan," she supplied.

The doorbell rang. He glared over his shoulder at the front door. What the hell was this, Grand Central Station?

"Hold on. There's someone at the door," he told her, crossing back to the living room.

"Yes, I know." She smiled at him as he opened the door. "It's me," she concluded brightly as they made eye contact.

Morgan punched the off button on the portable phone, then dropped his arm, still holding on to the unit. "Are you stalking me?" he said.

"No." Although it wasn't visible, she could have

sworn she detected a hint of a smile on his lips, one that he was fighting to hide. "It used to be called 'being concerned,'" she told him, closing her cell phone and slipping it into her pocket. "I was just passing by and saw the light."

He found that highly suspect. "How do you just 'pass by' a house in a residential community, especially if that house is at the end of a cul de sac?"

Undaunted, she said, "I could have friends in the neighborhood."

She was lying. And yet, she looked so innocent. He had a feeling that she made a hell of a poker player.

"Do you?"

"Depends." She raised her eyes to his in a movement that whispered of sex. The tourniquet around his stomach tightened again. "Are we friends?"

He heard himself laugh and was more surprised by the sound than she was. Morgan shook his head. "I've never been friends with a crazy person before."

The corners of her eyes crinkled as she smiled at him. The smile was warm, seductive, and it made him want to make love with her despite all the vows he'd made to the contrary.

"First time for everything," she told him. "How do you feel about weddings?"

The question knocked him for a loop. Damn woman did that on purpose, he thought, to see his reaction. "In general, specifically or my own?"

"Yes, yes and no." Before he could ask another question, Kelsey handed him a small, delicate off-white envelope with scalloped edges. His name and address were written in precise handwriting across the front. There was no return address and no postage affixed.

She watched him look the envelope over, as if he was debating even opening it. She saved him the trouble. "It's for Travis and Shana's wedding."

"Travis," he repeated, then shook his head. Why would he be invited to the wedding? "I'm not even sure which one of your brothers that is."

Kelsey laughed and quipped, "As long as Shana knows, that's all that's important." And then she became more serious. "My mother said to tell you that she'd really like you to attend."

Kate was a very nice woman, but why would she care one way or another if he attended. "Why?"

"Because she thinks you need to be around people a little more."

If anything, he'd welcome the reverse. "I *am* around people. Five days a week, I'm around more people than either you or she encounter."

"Happy people," Kelsey emphasized, "not people who are angry or hurt." She eyed him pointedly. "My mother likes to fix people."

Where the hell had that come from? And just what was she trying to tell him? "And you?" he asked.

He couldn't take his eyes off her mouth as a smile slowly unfurled on her lips. "They tell me I take after my mother."

He rather liked the woman's mother, but that didn't mean he was willing to give Kate Marlowe or her daughter a pass to meddle in any aspect of his life. He was fine just the way he was.

"Well, no disrespect to your mother intended, but I'm not broken."

The minute he said it, he could hear the trap snapping shut around him.

"Then attending shouldn't be a problem," Kelsey told him.

He laughed shortly. "I was doomed from the start, wasn't I?"

This time, he could almost taste her smile. Was this what an addict felt like, wanting something that wasn't any good for him?

"Pretty much. This really will mean a lot to Mom. To all of us."

He couldn't begin to understand why a group of relative strangers would care whether or not he showed up at a family wedding. But he had a feeling that if he really pushed for an answer, Kelsey would tell him. At length. It was much easier—and far more peaceful—just to go along with it. So he did.

He sighed. "I guess I can't say no."

"That's the general idea. Now that that's settled, can I see how the car's coming along?"

"Yeah, sure, why not?" At least he understood cars, he thought, taking refuge in the familiar.

Morgan led the way to his garage.

Chapter Twelve

"You have *no* idea how glad I am that you came," Kate told Morgan, clasping his hands between her own.

The wedding had been beautiful and the reception was being held at Trevor's restaurant, Kate's Kitchen. Trevor had named the establishment after her since she was the one responsible for his having enough nerve to follow his dream. Up to the point when he went off to culinary school, his father had been counting, none too secretly, on his becoming a lawyer and joining him in the firm along with Trent.

It had been a very hectic morning and afternoon and this was the first opportunity that Kate'd had to say something to Morgan that didn't revolve around instructions or dealing with yet another wedding emergency.

She sounded sincere, Morgan thought, and his mouth quirked in a half smile. Ordinarily, when he heard those words, it was because he'd arrived to help a citizen in some sort of trouble. Technically, he supposed that actually did apply here, seeing as how he'd had to step into someone else's shoes to prevent what Kate had called a "wedding disaster."

With a self-conscious shrug, he murmured something that sounded like "No problem."

Dressed in a full-length light blue dress, Kate looked more like the groom's older sister than someone old enough to be his mother.

Feeling a little emotionally and physically spent, Kate took a seat at the table.

"I don't know what we would have done if you hadn't stepped in at the last minute, taking William's place," she told him, her blue eyes sparkling. William Allen was to have been one of Travis's ushers, but according to Travis, he'd called last night to say that he'd tripped over his enthusiastic Great Dane and broken his arm. With profuse apologies, William had dropped out of the wedding party.

Morgan looked at Kelsey's mother. The half smile on his lips grew a tad larger. They both knew it was more of a matter of being "pushed" in than "stepping" in. For reasons that made no sense to Morgan, William's withdrawal had created a huge problem. Before he knew it, Kelsey asked if he minded taking William's place. Stunned, he'd said that yes, he did mind. Moreover, he had no desire to march down an aisle with a church full of strangers watching him.

He remembered Kelsey smiling indulgently at him. "No offense, Morgan, you are really good-looking and all, but that church full of people will be watching Shana. A couple of them might be watching Travis," she allowed, "but it's the bride who's the star at a wedding, not a groomsman. Still," she'd continued, "you do have the right to turn my mother down."

"Your mother?" Even as he spoke, he'd felt the trap closing around him. "I thought that I was turning you down."

"It's a package deal," she'd informed him. "And if you don't take William's place, I'm going to have to drop out of the wedding, too."

He'd tried to understand what one thing had to do with the other but failed. "Why?"

"We're short one groomsman," she'd reminded him. "So?"

"So," she'd elaborated, "Shana's a little superstitious about odd numbers."

Definitely a trap closing around him, he'd thought. But he wasn't about to agree to this without making Kelsey work for it. "Let me get this straight—if I say no, you don't get to be in it, either?"

She'd taken a breath and then released it in a heart-felt sigh. All that was missing, he remembered thinking, were violins. "You got it."

He debated making her twist a little longer, then decided there was no point to it. "All right, I'll do it," he'd agreed, then asked, "Does anyone ever get to win an argument with you?"

Kelsey had looked at him, the picture of wide-eyed innocence. "Happens all the time."

Good as she was at keeping a straight face, he hadn't believed it for a moment. "Let me know the next time it happens."

She'd laughed then and promised, "You'll be the first one to know," just before she threw her arms around his neck and kissed him to express her gratitude.

That had set the tempo for the rest of the evening.

As it turned out, Morgan was the same size as the former groomsman, so getting a tuxedo at the last minute hadn't posed a problem. Not that he'd actually figured it would. Somehow, between Kelsey and her mother, he had a feeling that they probably would have conjured one up if the present tux hadn't fit.

When it came right down to it, witchcraft was the only way to explain how he'd actually allowed himself to be roped into taking William's place. Not only roped into doing it—and this was the real kicker—but not minding it.

When it came right down to it, Morgan had no idea that witches came in size 4 or that they had hair that captured the rays of the sun and shone like spun gold in the late-afternoon sun.

In response to what Kate was saying to him, he shrugged again. "Kelsey would have roped someone else into taking that guy's place if I had turned her down."

"But you didn't turn her down," Kate pointed out. "And you made life a lot easier for all of us by saying yes."

As a policeman, he'd trained himself to pick up

nuances in a person's voice, and something in Kate's made him think she was leaving a lot more unsaid than said. His curiosity was aroused, but asking for an explanation would only get him further entrenched in a family affair. And although they acted like it, this *wasn't* his family. There was no sense in allowing himself to pretend—even for a moment.

He was an outsider and he always would be.

"Ah, there she is," Kate announced, looking past his shoulder.

He turned to see Kelsey weaving around the small tables, making her way to them. To him. If he'd been given to believing in fairy tales, she looked like one of the princesses so easily found in those stories. Except that, no matter what she said to the contrary, he had a strong feeling that Kelsey was not the type who would ever need rescuing.

But the prince might.

Kate rose the moment her daughter reached the table. "Does Trevor need any help in the kitchen?" she asked.

Kelsey shook her head. "He's got everything under control. He even asked Emilio to come in and take over so that he could enjoy Travis's wedding." Turning to Morgan, she said, "Emilio used to be Trevor's assistant chef until Trevor staked him to a restaurant of his own," she explained for his benefit. "It was hard on him, losing Emilio, but he knew that Emilio would never have enough nerve—or money—to go off on his own unless he pushed him out of 'the nest.'"

Morgan had learned, at an early age, that life was

hard and you had to take care of yourself because no one else would. He'd never thought that people like the Marlowes, people who went out of their way for others, actually existed.

"I need to say hello to Emilio," Kate said to him, excusing herself.

"Brace yourself," Kelsey called after her mother. "He's grown a beard." When she turned back to Morgan, she found him studying her. "What?"

"Are all you people do-gooders?" he asked.

Kelsey sat down at the table and took a sip from her wineglass. "What do you mean?"

He recounted just a few of the things he'd learned about the Marlowes since he'd met them. "That story about Trevor helping his assistant get his own restaurant, your father and Travis taking on cases pro bono, your mother and Trent treating patients for free if they couldn't afford to pay for sessions. Mike and Miranda setting up a foundation in her father's name to send inner-city kids to baseball games in the summer—"

She smiled, stopping him. "It's called giving back, Morgan. My family and I feel that we've been very lucky in our lives and we just want to share a little of our good fortune."

It occurred to him that she'd never said anything about her "extracurricular" activities. He knew she had to have some. "How do you 'share'?"

He could feel the warmth radiating from her as she smiled at him. "You mean other than finding lost souls and trying to reintegrate them into society?"

She obviously was referring to him. With a dismissive wave of his hand, he said, "Yes, other than that."

"I volunteer at a free clinic, helping kids with speech impediments and other problems." For a moment, her expression grew serious. "It takes so little to destroy a kid's self-esteem. I try to help them get it back." Suddenly, she stopped talking and turned to face the band her father had hired. She lit up like a Christmas tree right in front of him. "Oh, they're playing a song."

Morgan looked over his shoulder at the five men, one woman off to the side where a dance floor had been designated.

"They're a band." He pointed out. "They're supposed to be playing a song."

Kelsey was on her feet again, and he had a feeling he knew what was coming. Or, at least what she was going to ask. No way was he going to comply. Being part of the wedding party just involved walking a straight line. Dancing and making a fool of himself in public—and in front of her—was a completely different matter.

Kelsey wove her fingers through his and gave him what was easily a thousand-watt smile as she tugged on his hand. "Dance with me."

It wasn't a request, but it wasn't a demand, either, so he couldn't get annoyed. But neither did he move.

"I don't dance," he told her, remaining exactly where he was.

He could see by the light that came into Kelsey's eyes that she wasn't about to give up. "You can stand, can't you?"

He couldn't very well deny that. "Yeah," he answered warily.

"And you can sway, right? Just a little, like this," she illustrated by swaying her hips ever so slowly to the band's tempo. It was just enough to make his throat tighten.

"That's not dancing, that's being seductive," he told her.

Kelsey grinned as she tugged on his hand again, this time with a little more verve. "Potato, po-tah-to. The object is to have fun."

"I can have all the fun I can handle sitting down." To his surprise, for once, Kelsey said nothing. She just continued looking at him. After a minute, Morgan found himself capitulating. "Oh, all right, I'll stand up and sway."

The sound of her laughter, filled with delight and yet sexy as all hell, filled his head. "That's all I ask, Morgan."

"No, you're asking for a hell of a lot more than that and you know it," he told her.

And while she asked, she also eroded the ground that was beneath his feet, the foundation he'd put down when he'd finally, painstakingly, pulled his life back together. She was doing it one chipped piece at a time, but she was definitely doing it.

He knew he could stop dead, plant his feet on the floor and just stop moving. Stick of dynamite or not, she wasn't stronger than he was. But he didn't hold his ground. He allowed her to lead him to the dance floor, silently calling himself an idiot.

Reaching her destination, Kelsey turned around,

slipped her hands into his and lightly pressed her body against him.

Just enough to fan the flames that were already burning.

Kelsey turned her face up to his, the picture of innocence again. If innocence had a wicked glint in its eyes.

"See?" she asked. "This isn't so bad now, is it, Morgan?"

Bad? Yes, it was bad. Bad because it was damn near perfect—and something he could get accustomed to so very easily. He knew if he allowed that to happen, it would be a *really* bad thing because it meant that he would be in a vulnerable position. Again.

He knew that and yet, he couldn't make himself just walk away. Not yet.

"It's torture," he told her darkly, "but I guess I'll put up with it for now."

She smiled at him, her eyes lighting up and their warmth touching him in all the spots he'd long since thought were dead, or at least incapable of feeling anything.

"Ah, a sense of humor," she noted, delighted. "Nice to know I'm rubbing off on you a little."

Morgan laughed shortly and murmured something unintelligible.

The operative word here, he thought, being *rubbing*. Morgan could feel her body swaying against his, could really feel himself responding even though he didn't want to. There would be a price to pay for going along with her request, and in his gut he knew that he'd be paying it. Sooner than later.

But all he could think about right now was making love with her again, this even though he'd promised himself that it was never going to happen again.

Some willpower, he silently mocked himself.

It wasn't that he felt disloyal to his wife or anything nearly that uncomplicated. Mixed in with the urges and passions associated with desire that he felt was fear. A very strong, sinewy ribbon of fear. Fear that he was becoming vulnerable. That he could no longer protect himself.

He'd had his heart ripped out by the roots once when he'd lost Beth and their daughter. He never, *ever* wanted to be in that kind of position again. Never wanted to number among the walking wounded again, wanting only to die but knowing that he had to go on living, if for no other reason than to keep their memory alive. Because he was the only one left who remembered them.

It had taken a long time for it to stop hurting when he breathed.

And now along came this golden-haired woman with her laughing eyes and her soul-tempting mouth. She was breaking down his walls, was making him think about things that belonged in the life of a normal man, not the shell of a man he had become.

She was making him think about things he shouldn't yearn for. Because he knew that nothing ever lasted, and neither would she. Today, tomorrow, next week, or maybe even a little longer, but then she'd be gone. He'd be alone again, left to try to cope with an emptiness that hurt like hell.

He couldn't go through that another time.

"You look very good in a tuxedo," she said to him when the silence between them got to be too much. "The 'bad guys' would never recognize you."

Damn it, her body swaying against his that way was short-circuiting his brain, making it hard to concentrate, he thought. "Maybe I can use this as a disguise if I ever have to go undercover."

She laughed again, raising his body temperature several degrees. "It's a thought." Kelsey turned her face up to his. "What are you doing after the wedding?" she asked.

How much longer was this song going to go on? he wondered. "Going on with my life."

"In other words, nothing specific."

Morgan lifted one shoulder in a vague, noncommittal shrug. She went on looking at him. "Why, what did you have in mind?"

Her smile widened. How she pulled off wicked and innocent at the same time was beyond him, but she did. "I was hoping you'd have something in mind."

There was no skirting around her meaning. Morgan laughed and shook his head. Kelsey Marlowe was definitely one of a kind, he thought.

"You always been this shy?" he asked, amused.

She nodded solemnly. "It's a curse, but don't try to change the subject."

"Wouldn't dream of it." He could feel a quickening in his loins, a longing that was all too familiar in its demand. Unlike the handful of other women who had passed through his life since he'd lost Beth, one taste of Kelsey hadn't satisfied anything. It had just led him to wanting another. And another. There was no point in pretending otherwise. "Your place or mine?"

"Whichever's closer," Kelsey breathed. She moved in closer, doing away with the last bit of space between them.

"Don't they look good together?" Kate asked.

She was dancing with her husband, but her attention was completely focused on Kelsey and Morgan. She hadn't taken her eyes off the couple since Kelsey had dragged Morgan out onto the dance floor.

Bryan glanced in his daughter's direction. "Yes, they do," he agreed. When he looked back at his wife, something suddenly dawned on him, highlighted in big neon lights. "William Allen didn't break his arm yesterday, did he?" he asked suspiciously.

Kate didn't give him a direct answer. "Why would he call to say he did if he didn't?"

He knew her by now, knew that Kate never lied. She did know how to use words in such a way as to suggest things without actually saying them. She was exceedingly clever, he mused, offering nonanswers in place of actual answers.

"I'm the lawyer here, Kate. I'm the one who's supposed to twist words around."

She was the personification of innocence as she asked, "Whatever do you mean, Bryan?"

He bent over to whisper into her ear. "Come clean, Kate."

Rather than continue the verbal dance, she laughed

softly. When Bryan straightened his head, Kate smiled up into his eyes.

"You always could see right through me, couldn't you?" As they continued dancing, she filled him in on what had really happened. "When I saw William yesterday at the tuxedo rental shop, he looked very unhappy. I managed to get him to tell me what was wrong. He said his wife didn't want him being part of the wedding party without her. William didn't want to hurt Travis's feelings, but he didn't want to upset his wife and have her complaining for the entire night, either. I just gave him a way out."

"Out of the altruistic goodness of your heart," Bryan declared with a deadpan expression.

She knew that Bryan saw through her, but there was a comfort in having your spouse know you so well that he could finish your thoughts. She took solace in that closeness. "You know how good my heart is, Bryan."

"Yes," he whispered with all sincerity, "I do."

As he danced, Bryan pressed his hand to the small of her back, thinking how delicate and petite Kate felt against him. He'd almost forgotten that she was pregnant and that all this would soon change. That petite little body he knew so well would be rounded out with their child. Desire, roused by emotion, suddenly filled him.

He found himself looking forward to the night ahead, after the reception was over and Travis and Shana were off on their honeymoon. It was time to recreate a little of their own honeymoon. Most men, after twenty-seven years of marriage, just went through the motions. But he was more in love with his wife than ever. Bryan knew he was one of the lucky ones.

Chapter Thirteen

He was happy.

These past few years, happiness had become such a foreign concept to Morgan that it had taken him almost a month to recognize it. Being with Kelsey, looking forward to seeing her, even to interacting with her family, all of this made him happy. Quietly, subtly, supremely happy.

But recognition and admission inevitably reintroduced the specter of fear.

Against his will, Morgan found himself waiting for the other shoe to drop. For the happiness to abruptly end without warning, like a bomb being thrown at him—the way it had last time—and sending him plummeting back into the dark, lonely world he'd inhabited before his path had crossed Kelsey's.

All things ended. And this would, too. Most likely when he was least prepared for it.

The best way to handle it would be on his own terms. The only way to be braced for it would be if he just walked away from it while there still was an "it." That way, he wouldn't be sucked into an abysmal vortex when happiness was no longer part of his life.

The description might be melodramatic, but he knew damn well that if he wasn't prepared, when happiness vacated his life, he *would* be broadsided, like a Middle Ages galleon receiving a lethal blow below its water line.

After being devastated by his mother's death and then his father's steady descent into a depression that placed the man far beyond his reach, Morgan never thought that life would have a purpose, a real reason for him to live, until Beth had made him feel otherwise. Beth had been his secret source of strength, his reason to smile. When the baby came along, his life was absolutely complete.

He'd been so foolish then, thinking things had finally turned around for him. He'd been supremely happy with his little corner of the world.

Life taught him that things could change in a blink of an eye.

But even knowing what could—and most likely *would*—happen, knowing how devastating the loss would be, he had still allowed his barriers to begin crumbling. Still found himself looking forward to seeing Kelsey, still allowed himself to be absorbed into the fabric of her family.

He'd gotten too comfortable, Morgan chided himself. And that was exactly when disaster always struck. It waited for complacency, for happiness to blot out everything else, making a man myopic, and then it struck, just because it could, stripping him of everything. Leaving him bent and bleeding, going through the motions and having no real reason to go on living.

He had to back away, for his own preservation.

Like with a bandage that had gotten stuck to a wound, he had to rip it away cleanly. It would hurt, but pulling it off slowly would hurt even more, only prolonging the pain.

"You're quieter than usual," Kelsey commented, turning toward Morgan in bed. They had just made love and his silence made the afterglow slip into the shadows quicker than it should.

She felt herself growing uneasy.

As with so many nights since her brother's wedding, they had gotten together for no particular reason, with no set agenda, just to see each other. In the beginning, the get-togethers occurred aided by excuses. She would invite Morgan to a movie, or he would suggest going to a restaurant, when all either of them really wanted was just to enjoy the other's company.

But after a while, the excuses no longer seemed necessary. It was enough that they just wanted to see one another.

At least, she'd thought that it was enough. But the past few days Morgan had become pensive. More so than usual. Kelsey vacillated between giving Morgan his space and wanting to take on whatever was bothering him to make his burden lighter.

Not knowing what was going on in his head had her thinking all sorts of things were wrong.

He sat up. "Just thinking," he murmured with a careless shrug that wasn't reassuring. Telling herself that she was just imagining things didn't help, either.

"Yes, I can see the wheels turning." Kelsey glided a finger along his temple as if she were able to access his thoughts at will. If only it were that simple. "There's this little vein that becomes prominent whenever you're lost in thought," she told him, then asked, "Anything I can help with?" fervently hoping that whatever was bothering him had nothing to do with the two of them.

"Or is it police stuff?" she asked when he didn't respond. "And it's all based on 'need to know'?" Kelsey uttered the phrase with disdain.

Morgan shook his head. "No," he said. And then he slanted a look in her direction, his expression unreadable. "Just something I need to work out."

She didn't like the sound of that. Or his low tone. It made her feel uneasy, although she couldn't really explain why.

"If you share a burden, it's always lighter," she said, trying to sound chipper.

"Not always," he countered. If he'd let her in, told her what was really on his mind before he acted on it, she might misunderstand. She might think it was her fault, or worse, that she could somehow magically "fix the problem."

Kelsey was quiet for a moment, scrutinizing him. "Does this have anything to do with us?" she asked.

Us. Two little letters. They sounded so solid, so good. But he knew how quickly that could all change, dissolving to nothingness.

In response, Morgan merely shrugged his shoulders and looked away.

A chill ran down her spine. He wasn't answering her. She'd thought—hoped—that she was making him happy. At the very least half as happy as he made her. In her wildest dreams, she'd never known that she could be this in love. Corny as it sounded, it took everything she had not to just burst into song at the drop of a hat.

She was *that* happy.

And she had clung to the hope that the feeling could go on indefinitely, evolving into a permanent connection. She'd asked for no "talks," made no attempt to back him into a corner to "define" their relationship in any manner, shape or form. She'd been determined not to make him feel any pressure. And, in deference to Morgan, she'd deliberately bitten back the words "I love you" whenever they had sprung to her lips, even though it was happening with more frequency these last couple of weeks.

There was no denying that she really was in love with Morgan.

She hadn't thought such feelings were possible. But love had hit her hard. She hadn't said a word, hadn't even hinted at it, because she was afraid that she'd frighten Morgan away, or at least make him take a few steps back. She'd been fairly confident that she could wait Morgan out until he was ready to make his own declaration to her.

In the weeks since Trent and Shana's wedding, she'd witnessed a steady change in Morgan, one she wasn't sure he was even aware of. It had given her hope. Morgan had been steadily lightening up. A few times, after they'd made love, she'd actually caught him smiling, just smiling to himself. It was a very good sign.

But right now, it was as if none of that had happened. He was changing again, and this time it was a reversal of attitude. The ground they'd gained now seemed to be breaking apart.

Maybe she was wrong. Maybe, in her concern that Morgan would shift back to the way he'd been initially, she read too much into his expression, into his pensive manner.

Everyone had an off day, an off week, right?

Even as she told herself that, a chill wrapped around her heart.

He loved her. She *knew* that, was certain of it. And yet…

There was a way to put that to the test, Kelsey thought. Mentally, she squared her shoulders and banked down the sudden wave of fear that threatened to wash over her.

She tried to sound nonchalant as she said, "Did I tell you I got an offer the other day?"

"An offer?" Morgan repeated, not sure where she was going with this. "You mean like someone propositioned you?"

She tried to laugh, but the situation was suddenly way too serious.

"No, not like that," she told him. "I'm talking about a job offer."

His expression continued to be unreadable. "I thought you said you were happy where you are."

"I am," she assured him quickly. She didn't want him to think that she was the one who was dissatisfied, who was restless. "I didn't go looking for this, it just came up." Kelsey realized that she wasn't making any sense and backed up. "A friend of my mother's brought my name up to this headmaster who has an opening coming up in his school. It would be teaching in a private school." Why did she feel so shaky? She wasn't making any of this up, yet she tripped over her tongue. Did he detect the tremor in her voice? "I'd be working with kids who have special needs," she added.

"Don't you do that now?" he asked.

"Up to this point, I've only done it on a limited basis. This would be an entire small class of kids with special needs," she said, watching his face for any sort of reaction.

He merely nodded his head. "Sounds noble."

"I'm not noble," she contradicted. Tense, she'd almost snapped at him. "I would, however, be helpful. I did help get through to Trent's son—before he was Trent's son," she qualified.

It was the first sign of interest she saw in his face. "Cody's not his son?"

She realized that no one had told him—and Cody had the same hair color and complexion as Trent so it was easy to see why Morgan had just made the logical assumption. When they were together, Trent and Cody behaved as if they were father and son.

"No, he's Laurel's. Cody was in the car when his father died in a car accident. Cody didn't talk for a year. Laurel tried to help him come around, but nothing worked. She finally turned to Trent at his practice for help and he asked me to see what I could do to get the boy's grades up again."

Morgan thought of the animated boy he'd met. It was hard to think of Cody as withdrawn in any fashion. "So you're good at this sort of thing," he surmised.

Cody had been her greatest accomplishment to date and she was proud of how he'd overcome his obstacles. But she minimized her effect on him now with a shrug. "Fairly good," she allowed.

"So what's the problem?" Morgan asked, not understanding her dilemma. "Take the job if you think you'll like it."

She took a breath before answering. "The job is in New York."

"Oh."

Kelsey took solace from the single word, more so than she knew she should. But a drowning woman clutched at anything, praying that it would turn into a life preserver.

"Yes, 'oh.'" She waited for Morgan to say more. When he didn't, she prodded him a little by asking, "What do you think I should do?"

He turned it right back on her. "What do you want to do?"

Now he sounded just like a psychologist, she thought, frustrated. Was it just to get her to examine her motives in considering the position—or was this a way for him to step out of her life without incurring any sort of battle scars?

"I'm not sure," she answered quietly. "I'm having trouble deciding," she added. Sitting up in bed, she pulled her knees in against her, as if to gather strength. "Don't you have an opinion?"

He didn't tell her what she wanted to hear. "It's your life, Kelsey," he pointed out, his voice devoid of emotion. "Ultimately, you have to do what you think is best for you."

That sounded so distant, so clinical, Kelsey thought. So cold.

From out of nowhere, tears gathered in the corner of her eyes. For a moment, she looked away, struggling to regain control over herself.

It wasn't working.

Kelsey could feel her very spirit draining out of her. Leaning her head against her knees, she continued averting her eyes from his. "I guess then I should fly out for an interview. Explore my options."

"Sounds like a plan," he agreed, his voice still flat.

Yeah, a plan to be rid of me, she thought angrily. Didn't he care if she left? Or was he hoping she would because things between them had gotten too complicated, too intimate?

She almost shouted the question at him, but somehow managed to keep the words to herself. Letting him see how much his indifference hurt wouldn't get her anywhere. Even if he felt guilty about it, she didn't want him sticking around out of pity or guilt. She wanted him to ask her to stay because he loved her. Love was the only reason for anything to happen.

She'd been fooling herself. Morgan didn't love her. If he did, he'd be trying to convince her to stay, saying *something* to show her that he cared.

Damn it, she would have sworn that there were feelings between them, that he loved her, at least *cared* about her even though he wasn't vocal about it.

Now she knew better.

Her arms tightened around her knees. How long had he been planning his escape, hoping for something to come along that would be instrumental in a breakup between them?

Kelsey felt sick.

"Listen," she turned to look at him, "I'm not feeling all that well right now."

Morgan was quick to take his cue. There was too much emotion in the room, too much for him to deal with. He didn't know how much longer he could remain stoic like this.

"Yeah," he nodded, "I should be going. I've got some things I've been meaning to get to."

"At nine-thirty at night?" she questioned.

"Yeah, well…" Instead of continuing, searching for something plausible to say, Morgan swung his legs out of the bed and got up.

Ordinarily she liked watching him get out of bed. Liked watching him move in strong, measured, steady steps, a sleek panther that was the undeniable ruler of all he saw. But right now, she couldn't bring herself to look at him. It hurt too much. There was absolutely no comfort in the fact that she'd been right all along. That falling for Morgan would only bring her heartache.

Gathering his clothes together from the chair where he'd haphazardly tossed them as their heated kisses had given way to lovemaking, Morgan held them against him and turned to look at her now.

"When would you be leaving?"

Kelsey searched for a drop of warmth, of concern, of resistance to the idea in his voice.

There was none.

"I don't have the job yet," she pointed out stiffly, her voice all but muffled. "The head of the school would have to interview me first."

"That's what I mean," he told her. His voice sounded a little strained. Did it annoy him to have to talk to her? "When would you fly out for the interview?"

She had to think to form an answer. "I'm not sure yet. He gave me a number of alternative dates."

Morgan nodded, taking in the information. "If you get a chance, let me know when."

If you get a chance.

You would say this to a neighbor who asked you to bring in their mail. You *wouldn't* sound so cavalier with someone you had feelings for.

There was a simple explanation. He *didn't* have feelings for her. It had all been one-sided with her reading much too much meaning into everything.

You'd think that after what she'd gone through with Dan, she would have learned her lesson. She'd held Morgan at bay for how long? A day? Two? A week? It was all a blur to her now because her feelings had been there from the beginning. All she knew was that they'd quickly become lovers.

She'd always worn her heart on her sleeve, Kelsey thought contemptuously. Added to that, she'd thought she'd seen something in him, a wounded human being who needed to make contact with someone who cared about him.

That was what she *thought* she saw, Kelsey upbraided herself. For all she knew, it had all been an act. An act he put on to get her to break down her barriers so that he could sleep with her. It had been about sex, pure and simple. Just sex and nothing else. Whatever she'd thought was there wasn't.

Wrapping the sheet around herself like an overly long toga, she got out of bed and followed Morgan, now fully dressed, to the door. All she wanted now was to be rid of him before she started to cry.

"Give me a call if you get a chance," he reminded her, reaching the door. "Let me know when you're going to New York."

"Sure," she murmured, completely numb inside. She shut the door without saying goodbye.

What was wrong with him? the voice in her head cried. He was supposed to ask her not to even *think* about leaving. He was supposed to beg her to stay, or at least act as if he would miss her. Instead, he was encouraging her to go, to consider uprooting her life and moving three thousand miles away.

God, she never thought she could hurt this much.

Kelsey leaned her forehead against the door, her head throbbing as the tears began to flow. She could feel herself dying inside.

Damn him, anyway!

With effort, she straightened again and slowly moved away from the door. She needed to get a grip on herself.

But first, she needed to go back into her bedroom, throw herself on the bed and cry until she stopped hurting.

On the other side of the door, Morgan finally allowed his rigid posture to relax, his shoulders to slump. Now that he was faced with the sound of the second shoe falling, he wanted to take it all back, wanted to grab it before it made contact with the floor.

He didn't want her to go. Oh God, he didn't want her to fly out for the interview, much less consider taking the job.

Get hold of yourself, Donnelly.

Better now than later, he thought after a beat. He knew this was for the best, both for her and for him, but as he slowly walked to his car, he couldn't find a way to overcome the sensation that he'd just had his heart cut out of his chest with a jagged knife.

Chapter Fourteen

He missed her.

God help him, but he missed her. Less than five days into the breakup and the loneliness was all but consuming him.

Morgan shifted in the car, his muscles cramping up on him as he sat, waiting, watching for close to an hour. Watching for her. He'd known this was going to be the ultimate outcome and had tried to put the skids on, stopping anything from happening before it had a chance to start.

Obviously, he'd wound up failing miserably. He was making matters worse by sitting here, parked across the street from the school where she taught, hoping to catch a glimpse of Kelsey as she left.

He'd succeeded only once in the past few days and it had only made things worse for him, not better.

Everything was making things worse, and soon, he knew, she'd be gone. Maybe even permanently if those people at the private school made her a decent offer.

By all rights, his life should have gone back to normal, or at least back to the way they had been before he'd met her, if that could be called normal.

No, he reflected, it hadn't been normal. Life before Kelsey had been hell. But he had made his peace with that.

Leaning forward in his seat, the steering wheel pressing into his chest, Morgan thought he saw her coming out of the school's main building. Just then, his radio crackled, summoning his attention.

Banking down his impatience, he flicked the button down and listened. Dispatch was calling, alerting him to a possible break-in taking place three miles away. A neighbor had reported a suspicious-looking truck parked across the street from her house.

Sighing, he reached for the radio's receiver and responded. "Did the caller identify herself?"

"No," the dispatch officer on the other end of the line told him. "And how did you know it was a 'she'?"

"Because, ten to one, if the suspicious truck is parked on Deerwood, it belongs to a plumber paying a call on Mrs. Wilson again." He recited an address that he had been to before.

"The caller said the truck has been parked there all day and that it was parked there all day yesterday, as well. According to her, no work's being done."

He'd talked to the owner of the truck the last time this had been called in. Nothing illegal was going on. "Most likely Mr. Wilson is away on a business trip," Morgan replied.

He heard a deep chuckle on the other end of the line. "And I take it that Mrs. Wilson's pipes need cleaning?" the dispatch officer asked.

"Something like that. It happened last month. And the month before that. Mr. Wilson flies to Washington, D.C., the last week of every month," Morgan told him. "The call's coming from a Jill Sellers. Sellers lives across the street and has no hobbies other than watching what her neighbors are doing. That and watching procedural crime shows on TV at night." The woman had proudly informed him that she was far better informed than the average citizen, thanks to the programs she faithfully watched.

"Maybe you still better check it out," the dispatch officer advised.

"That's what they pay me for," Morgan answered. He ended the call, then looked back toward the school entrance.

Kelsey was nowhere to be seen. With a suppressed sigh, Morgan started up his vehicle.

He'd better get used to that, he thought, driving away. It would be true soon enough.

For a minute, she thought she saw him. A squad car had been parked across the street when she walked out of school and her heart leaped. She thought it was

Morgan. Thought that perhaps he'd finally decided to talk her out of going to New York.

Stupid. She looked up and down the block. The squad car was gone. *The man just isn't that into you.*

She had yet to fly out for the interview, but the impression she had gotten when she spoke to the headmaster, Philip Gilchrist, over the phone was that the interview was just a formality. The job was hers. Even before he'd extended the formal invitation to her, he'd spoken to the principal of her school and to some of her teachers at college. Gilchrist had told her that they had glowing things to say about her as a teacher and as a person. Sight unseen, she'd impressed him, especially because he knew some of her professors personally and had a great deal of respect for their opinions.

Gilchrist had gone on to say that, although he believed in crossing his *T*s and dotting his *I*s, he was fairly certain he knew the outcome of the face-to-face interview. In all probability, he was going to offer her the job.

All she had to do was say "yes."

He wasn't the one she wanted to say yes to, but life didn't always arrange itself the way people wanted, she thought ruefully.

The schoolyard was empty. All the children had been picked up. Kelsey went back inside the building to get her things. It was time to leave.

In more ways than one.

Kate sat very still as she listened to the voice on the other end of the line. Sensing that something was off and had been off for the past few weeks, she'd taken advantage of the break in her schedule to call Kelsey. She knew it was lunchtime over at the school where her daughter taught and she was hoping that Kelsey didn't have yard duty this week.

She didn't. But before Kate could ask her daughter if there was anything wrong or unusual going on, Kelsey had said, "I'm glad you called, Mom. I've been meaning to call you." And then there'd been a hesitation on the line before Kelsey asked, "How are you doing?"

Kate knew Kelsey referred to the pregnancy. She also knew that this was just a stall tactic. Something else was on her daughter's mind.

"I'm fine, honey. I don't feel like throwing up first thing in the morning anymore, which makes your father very happy. I think he was beginning to take it personally." She laughed softly. "How are you doing?" she asked.

"Fine. Okay."

The response was completely automatic and completely unconvincing. Her mother antennae shot up. She *knew* something was wrong. "Kelsey, I've known you all your life. You never could lie. Now tell me what's wrong."

"Nothing's wrong." The pause ran on too long. And then Kelsey said rather quickly, "I'm just probably going to change schools."

Kate knew how happy her daughter was teaching at her current elementary school. What had changed that? "Did you get a better offer?" she guessed to keep the dialogue moving.

"In a way."

Kate was instantly attuned to what wasn't being said. "And in what way isn't it a better offer?"

There was another pause, long enough to make Kate uneasy. "Well, I'd have to move."

Because Kelsey knew she could always rely on her family's help, Kate surmised that the physical act of moving from one place to another wasn't the problem. When Kelsey didn't elaborate, Kate asked, "How far a move?"

Kate was surprised that she had to prod Kelsey. Getting information out of her daughter had never felt like pulling teeth before.

"Pretty far," Kelsey answered.

"How far is 'pretty far'?"

She heard Kelsey taking a breath before saying, "I'd be moving to New York."

"New York?" Kate repeated incredulously. "You mean the city?"

Instantly, Kate felt torn. Mother birds were supposed to prepare their young to be ready to leave the nest and fly off on their own. But she dearly loved the fact that all of her children lived practically within shouting range. And Kelsey had moved out of the house only a few months ago. She was still trying to get used to Kelsey not being there in the morning, using up all the hot water, muttering under her breath about running behind schedule.

"Is this something you really want to do?" Kate pressed.

"Well, the offer came in last month and when I spoke to the headmaster he sounded eager to have me join the staff. He said the interview would pretty much be just a formality, and that if I decided I wanted it, the job was mine." Her voice gained speed as she spoke. "The salary's better because it costs more to live in New York City than it does here. I'd say it was pretty much the same salary—"

"You're not answering the question, Kelsey," Kate told her gently. "Is going to New York City to teach something that you really want to do?"

"Well, strictly speaking," Kelsey hedged, "I don't want to leave you with the baby coming and all. But I'll make sure I can get a leave of absence to fly back and help you when the big day comes."

That still wasn't answering her question. Kelsey wasn't excited. She wasn't taking a job—she was fleeing. Kate felt it in her bones. "Kelsey, sweetheart, what's wrong?"

"Nothing's wrong, Mom," Kelsey insisted a little too adamantly. "It's just time for me to leave the nest, that's all."

"The nest, I can see. You've already done that," she reminded her. "But the state?" Kate paused, waiting. "How does Morgan feel about your going?"

Kelsey struggled not to let her emotions get the better of her. Her mother had enough to deal with without having a daughter unloading on her.

"I doubt if he feels anything at all, Mom," she answered. "He said the decision was mine."

"Maybe Morgan doesn't want to influence you or make you feel that he's ruining a big chance for you."

"No, it's nothing that noble," Kelsey assured her. "I

really don't think it matters to him one way or another." And then she revised her statement. "Actually, I think he looked rather relieved when he heard I was thinking about going out for an interview."

"I don't believe that, Kelsey."

"You didn't see him when I told him," Kelsey pointed out. Her voice cracked at the end of the sentence. Kelsey pretended to clear her throat.

She needn't have bothered. Kate was well versed in Kelsey-speak and she had already picked up on the small, telltale signs in both her daughter's voice and the way she'd said what she had. Kelsey was hurt, very hurt, by what she perceived as Morgan's indifference. Kate strongly doubted that the patrolman was indifferent. He was undoubtedly still just struggling to deal with his growing feelings for her daughter. Most likely, when Kelsey had mentioned possibly moving to New York, he took that to mean she was leaving him and his sense of self-preservation had kicked in.

Just the way it had with Bryan all those years ago, Kate remembered. At the time he had been a widower falling in love for the first time since his wife had died. His fear of being hurt again had almost caused her to leave him.

"Don't you think you should talk to him again?" Kate suggested gently.

"No point, Mom," Kelsey said briskly, fighting the urge to break down and tell her mother how badly she ached inside. Her mother was always a huge comfort, but Kelsey wasn't a little girl anymore. She couldn't come running to her mother every time she fell down and scraped her knees. Or her heart. "Look, I have to go. I promise I won't just disappear into the night. I'll keep you updated."

"And when are you going for the interview?" Kate asked.

A round-trip ticket sat on her bureau. "I'm flying out Friday morning."

Friday morning. Today was Wednesday. That gave her very little time to pull off a miracle, Kate thought. "Come to dinner tomorrow night," she invited before Kelsey had a chance to hang up.

"Can't. I have too much to do." She had a feeling that if she came to dinner, her mother would have everyone else there to try to talk her out of going. And because she really didn't want to go, she would be an easy mark. She needed to get this moving. "We'll talk," Kelsey promised again.

The line went dead.

Kate replaced the receiver in its cradle. If Kelsey was thinking about taking the job in New York because she felt that this move would be good for her career or she'd always wanted to live in New York City, she would have hidden her disappointment, wished her daughter well and been glad for her.

But Kelsey *wasn't* doing this because the city held allure for her or the job was a once-in-a-lifetime opportunity. She was hurt and needed to lick her wounds far away from the cause of those wounds.

Kate squared her shoulders. Not if she had anything to say about this. To Kate, silence had always been love's worst enemy. It was time to pull her daughter and Morgan into a meaningful dialogue.

Moving her computer screen so that she could look at it better, Kate punched in the code to open her appointment schedule for the afternoon. She needed to make a few changes.

"Hey, there's somebody to see you, Donnelly," one of the patrolman said as he walked into the locker room. He jerked his thumb toward the entrance door. "Nice-looking lady."

Morgan instantly thought of Kelsey. The next moment, he scolded himself for allowing his hopes to get the better of him. Kelsey was out of his life.

He'd had just finished changing out of his uniform and into his civilian clothes. Shutting his locker, he asked the other man, "You get a name?"

The patrolman shook his head. "I would have gotten a number if I could have. But she wouldn't give me a name, said she just needed to talk to you. Some guys've got all the luck," the man lamented enviously as he crossed to his own locker.

Morgan frowned. He had to stop letting his imagination get the better of him. This was probably just some citizen he'd dealt with earlier. His shift was over for the day and he had been thinking about what to do with himself until it was time to come in again tomorrow. Life had just become a string of minutes that had no meaning and led nowhere.

He supposed that talking to his visitor was a good

way to stall. God knew nothing waited for him at home. He'd dropped Kate's car off at her house yesterday, while she and her husband were at work, getting one of the officers to bring him back to the precinct. That left him nothing to work on, nothing to do but think.

He didn't want to think.

"See you tomorrow," the patrolman called out to him as he walked out.

"Yeah," Morgan muttered.

And then he froze.

It wasn't just some citizen waiting to speak to him. It was Kate.

Had something happened to Kelsey? Then he remembered. She was probably here to thank him for dropping off the car. The blanket of disappointment almost suffocated him.

"Mrs. Marlowe, what are you doing here?" he asked. She seemed concerned. "Is there something wrong with the car?"

"No, the car is wonderful," she said, a quick smile curving her mouth. "It actually runs better now than when it was new." Reaching up, she placed her hand on his shoulder. "You're a magician." The embarrassed smile that flashed across his face belonged to the boy she knew he must have once been.

He watched her. *Was* this about Kelsey after all? He reined in his thoughts, trying not to get carried away without further input. "Then if it's not about the car, why—"

"Because I'm going to do something I don't ordinarily do." She looked around. They were right in front of the locker room and what she wanted to say required a little privacy. "Is there somewhere we can go that's out of the way?"

Private by nature, he definitely didn't want anyone overhearing his conversation with Kate. He suggested, "We could sit in my car."

She smiled. "That'll be fine."

As they left the building, Kate surprised him by hooking her arm through his. She began talking again.

"I don't believe in butting into my children's lives," she told him. "But I really can't just stand off to the side and watch, either. Because of my profession, I feel I have to speak up—especially when I'm watching a train about to be derailed."

Reaching his car, Morgan unlocked it and held open the passenger door for her. He'd said nothing while they were walking, but now he felt he needed to tell her that she needn't waste her breath. Kelsey was doing what she wanted to do, and that involved leaving him.

"Mrs. Marlowe—"

Kate raised her hand to silence him as she sat down. "Let me speak first, Morgan, and then you can protest all you want."

Rounding the hood, Morgan got in on the driver's side. He closed the door and shut out the rest of the world. "Go on."

"The pursuit of happiness is guaranteed under the Constitution," Kate began. "What the Constitution *doesn't* tell you is what to do about it if you have the great fortune to actually stumble across that happiness." She smiled, shaking her head. "It doesn't happen nearly as often as the movies and song writers would like to have us think it does." She shifted slightly in her seat. "I have always believed that if someone is lucky enough to encounter happiness, he or she should do everything in their power to hang on to it, not just let it go because something 'might' go wrong." She looked at Morgan pointedly.

She had no knowledge of the words that had been spoken between Morgan and her daughter, but given what he had gone through, she could guess. Especially because she had lived through it with Bryan herself.

By Morgan's expression, she could see that she'd guessed right.

"By walking away," Kate continued, "that becomes a self-fulfilling prophecy and you *make* it go wrong. I've watched you and Kelsey together. You fit," she told him simply. "You make each other happy—not an easy feat where Kelsey is concerned, I might add." She smiled fondly. "My daughter is headstrong and, although I love her dearly, I am aware of her flaws. She is *not* the easiest person to live with.

"But Kelsey lights up whenever you're around." Kate placed her hand on his, making contact, silently offering Morgan a bridge from his world into hers—and her daughter's. "And I've noticed that the same goes for you." She paused for a moment, looking into his eyes. Searching for a sign that she had gotten through to him.

"Don't throw all that away because of some misguided notion you have that you can protect your heart if you don't allow yourself to care," she implored. "You're only condemning yourself to a life of emptiness."

Taking a breath, she waited for him to speak.

*Kate's other daughter, she implored, "You won't
leave. You won't make us suffer..."
Instead, again she waited for them to speak.*

Chapter Fifteen

When the silence continued to drag on, Kate leaned over in her seat and softly prompted, "You can talk now, Morgan."

He was accustomed to maintaining his distance, or had been until Kelsey and her family changed all that. They had just invaded his space as if they belonged there. As if he was one of them and belonged in their world and they in his. Pretending otherwise, especially to Kate, seemed like a futile thing to do. He had a feeling Kelsey's mother could see past the smoke and mirrors, could see the hurt he felt.

"Is she really leaving?"

"That's what she says," Kate answered. "The flight's

tomorrow morning." She glanced at her watch. "She's home, packing. Give her a reason not to."

If Kelsey was packing, then she *wanted* to go. He had no right to stand in her way. "Mrs. Marlowe, maybe this is all for the best. She can do better."

Why were men so stubbornly pigheaded? Kate wondered in affectionate exasperation.

"No," Kate said emphatically, "she can't. From where I'm standing, my daughter is about to walk away from someone very special." She covered his hand with hers for emphasis, driving the point home. "And so are you. If I were strong enough, I'd get you both in the same room and knock your heads together. But I'm not, so I'm going to have to rely on the fact that you both are reasonably intelligent people who'll see the light if I can just get you to turn your heads in the right direction."

Finished, Kate looked at him expectantly. She had done all she could. The next move, they both knew, was his.

You would think that by now, Kelsey thought, no part of her still believed in fairy tales. All that "finding the right man" and "living happily ever after" really was a fairy tale.

Okay, her parents had a wonderful marriage, but that was rare and the result of luck more than anything else. Luck that her brothers had scared off not one, not two, but three nannies in relatively short order, throwing her father into a state of panic that had him virtually trolling for nannies. Luck that he'd brought Mike to a neighborhood party instead of sending him off on his own because it was so close by. Luck that her mother had picked *that particular party* to entertain and work her magic. And even more luck that her mother had been a starving student having progressively more and more trouble making ends meet.

If any of that hadn't happened, *she* wouldn't have happened and there wouldn't have been this wonderful, long-term marriage to look back on as part of her background.

Maybe, Kelsey thought, tossing a black pencil skirt into the suitcase laying open on her bed, if her parents had been divorced, she wouldn't have grown up looking at life through rose-colored glasses. She wouldn't have seen marriage as a haven. Moreover, she would have seen the world with all its warts and blemishes and *known* that losing her heart to a man was a huge mistake.

That jerk who'd said that it was better to have loved and lost than never to have loved at all didn't know what the hell he was talking about, she thought resentfully, flinging in several pairs of underwear. The "lost" part hurt like hell.

Damn it, tears meshed into her lashes, sliding down her cheeks.

Annoyed, Kelsey stopped flinging clothes and wiped the tears away with the back of her hand. He wasn't worth them.

If he wasn't worth the tears, there wouldn't have been any tears. She certainly wouldn't be shedding them now.

Her head ached. She wasn't making any sense anymore.

God, but she felt like exploding. If she didn't vent soon—

Kelsey grabbed the book she kept on her nightstand in hopes of eventually finishing it and flung it as hard as she could against the opposite wall. The noise that was made when it made contact with the wall wasn't nearly loud enough.

Her frustration didn't abate, even an iota.

She needed something heavier, something more substantial to throw, she thought angrily. Like a stack of dishes, one by one.

Or Morgan.

Kelsey took in a deep, cleansing breath and then let it out slowly. It helped. For approximately five seconds. So she took another. Just as the doorbell rang.

She glared toward the front of the house. Now what?

The doorbell rang a second time. Then a third. No sooner had the sound of insistent chimes died away than the knocking started. The knocking soon gave way to pounding. Hard pounding that threatened to bring down her front door.

The scenario was all too familiar. A couple of months ago, she'd been the one pounding on Morgan's door. Was this Morgan? Had he suddenly come around?

Stop it, Kelsey, she thought. *It's not Morgan. It's probably just some kid, selling subscriptions for his school.*

She wouldn't be here to read any magazines.

Deciding to ignore whoever was out there, she went back to packing. For all of ninety seconds.

There was no way to ignore the pounding as it grew increasingly louder. Whoever was out there must have huge, hard fists. It sounded as if he could go on pounding indefinitely.

Marching out of the bedroom, she crossed to the front door and swung it open. "I'm not interested!" she yelled and then froze.

It wasn't someone selling subscriptions.

It was Morgan.

"Well, I am!" he shouted back at her. His eyes blazed as they swept over her. "Don't you know any better than to open your door without looking to see who it is?" he demanded.

His anger made her forget what he'd first shouted at her. Forget to ask just what he meant. If he wanted a fight, damn it, he was going to get one. Tossing her head, she lied. "I knew it was you."

He didn't believe her. "How?" he demanded.

He hadn't told anyone where he was going, although he had a feeling that Kate had probably guessed he was coming to see Kelsey. Still, his gut told him that she wouldn't have said anything to her daughter, wanting her to be caught off guard.

Kelsey's mind raced as she tried to come up with an answer to back up her claim. "The pounding sounded familiar."

He stared at her. "I never pounded on your door," he reminded her. "You pounded on mine, remember?"

"No," she shot back. She was so angry at his presumption in coming here she couldn't think straight.

Didn't he realize that she was trying to get over him? Was he here to just jerk her around, to see if she still cared? "I am trying to forget everything about you."

Kelsey stopped abruptly, blowing out a breath. Everything she'd promised herself about her behavior if their paths should ever cross again had just gone out the window.

"Sorry," she said in a much more subdued voice. She was better off pretending to be indifferent than angry if she wanted to get back at him. "I didn't mean to shout. I just get edgy when I have a lot to do in a short amount of time."

"And what is it that you're trying to do in a short amount of time?" He knew the answer, but he hoped that if she was forced to say it out loud, maybe she would change her mind. On the way over, he'd decided that he was willing to try anything.

"Fly to New York." With that, she turned on her heel and walked back into her bedroom.

He could feel her words skewering his stomach. Pressing his hand to his belly as if to stem the flow of blood, he followed her.

The sight of the opened suitcase on the bed with clothing overflowing out of it pinched his gut even harder.

"So you're really going?" he heard himself ask.

"Sure. I'm exploring my options," she said, throwing his words back at him. "You know, what you told me to do when I asked you if I should go."

"I was trying to be impartial."

"Congratulations, you win the Impartiality Award of

the Year," she bit off sarcastically. "Should look very nice next to your Indifferent Award."

His eyes narrowed as he took in the accusation. "You think I'm indifferent?"

Kelsey raised herself up on her toes to be closer to his level. "I don't think—I know. You are," she declared.

He took a step into her space, his temper dangerously flaring. Kelsey stood her ground. "I'm indifferent about who wins the World Series. I'm indifferent about who wins the Super Bowl. I'm even indifferent about what brand of coffee I drink as long as it's strong and reasonably hot. I am *not* indifferent about you." Morgan fairly shouted at her now.

A sensible person might have taken this time to move back, or at least back off. Kelsey wasn't feeling very sensible right now.

"Ha!" she retorted, then turned away to continue packing.

Morgan grabbed her by her shoulders and turned her around to face him. "I didn't think I had the right to stand in your way if this was what you wanted."

She lifted her chin. "Nice speech, Donnelly. How long did it take you to convince yourself you were being noble instead of just running scared?"

His eyes narrowed even more. "You think that I'm scared?"

His eyes darkened. Another woman would have known that this wasn't the time to get into his face. But another woman wasn't on the verge of losing everything the way she was.

Kelsey tossed her head so that her blond hair went sailing over her shoulder. "Yes, I think you're scared. *Really* scared. Completely and utterly scared out of your mind."

"Of what?" His voice was low, dangerous.

She was out on a limb, but she wasn't about to crawl back to safety, not until she'd had her say. "Of caring again. I got to you, Morgan Donnelly." She jabbed a finger into his chest, emphasizing her point as she spoke. "For a very little while, I got to you," she jabbed him again, "and it scared the hell out of you."

He grabbed her finger before she could poke him a third time. "You're wrong."

"Am I?" she challenged pugnaciously.

"Yes." He continued to hold on to the offending finger, keeping it wrapped in his hand as he spoke. "You didn't get to me for a very little while—"

"I sure as hell—"

"For once in your life, will you shut up and listen?" he demanded, completely stunning her. "You didn't get to me for a very little while." He took a breath. "You got to me big-time. *That* was what scared me. Because my gut was twisting from wanting you. Because when we weren't together, I kept finding myself counting off the minutes until we were. You were becoming too important to me. You were my morning and my night. My reason for doing, for *being*.

"I don't like being dependent on anything." Opening his hand, he released her index finger. "I've seen what dependency does. My father was dependent on my mother and when she died, he slowly went to pieces. He was a good, decent man and he fell apart, bit by bit until there was nothing left.

"And I started going the same route after Beth and Amy died. I finally, *finally* was getting myself together, and then you happened. You are *nothing* like Beth, as different from her as night was from day, and yet, I can't breathe right without you around."

She wasn't going to let herself believe him, she wasn't, Kelsey kept repeating to herself in the confines of her mind. Just some huge disappointment waiting for her in the wings if she believed him.

"So you've been holding your breath ever since we broke up?" she asked, disbelief vibrating in every syllable.

"Yes, I have," he shot back. "And I can't do it anymore. I thought I could, that it would get better as the days went by, but it just got worse. I felt as if my gut had been cut out without the benefit of an anesthetic." He almost said "heart" instead of gut, but that would make him sound like some kind of wimp, and he wasn't. He was just a guy who'd been hurting too much for too long. Every day without her was an eternity.

She could almost picture that and it made her cringe. "Ouch."

"Yeah, 'ouch,'" he echoed.

Her eyes held his as she tried to figure out if she was being a fool to believe him or a fool not to.

"So you're telling me not to go?" she asked carefully.

In the last few days, he had become very aware of

words and the burden they brought with them. "I'm *asking* you not to go."

It occurred to Kelsey that, although it wasn't very PC of her, she wanted him to make the initial demand. To stand in her way, yelling that love was making him behave like this.

She was most likely losing her mind—and it was all his fault. "Why? Why are you asking me not to go?"

Uncomfortable, he shrugged, shoving his hands into his pockets. "Your family'll miss you."

"I'm not flying into the Bermuda Triangle. I'll be back."

"Your mother's pregnant. This is a difficult time for her. She needs you," he urged.

"Very sensitive of you," she said dismissively. "My mother has a whole support system in place. My father, my brothers, my sisters-in-law, they're all there for her. They can get her through this."

He shook his head. "That's not the same thing as a daughter."

"Granted, but again, I'll be back," she reminded him. Why was she doing this to herself? Why was she fishing for a response he wasn't prepared or willing to give her? "If she needs me, I can be back in five hours. Less if there's a strong tailwind."

"Sometimes," he told her slowly, "five hours just isn't fast enough."

Was he talking about a life-and-death situation? Her mother was the healthiest person she knew, but things could change quickly. "So now you're trying scare tactics to get me to stay?"

It was time to lower his shields. He realized it was his only chance. If that required making himself vulnerable, so be it. "I'll try anything I have to to get you to stay."

For a second, he'd left her speechless. "You know," she pointed out quietly, "there is a much simpler way to do that."

"What is it?"

Was he serious? Did he need a road map? Or was he just pulling her leg? "I'm not going to spell it out for you, Donnelly." But then she did. Sort of. "But it does involve three little words."

"Stay put, Kelsey?" he guessed, managing to keep a straight face.

"Try again," Kelsey prompted.

He took her into his arms, but he still didn't say what she wanted to hear. "This isn't easy for me, Kelsey."

"If it came easily to you, it wouldn't mean anything."

Holding Kelsey at arm's length, Morgan looked at her for a long moment. "And if I say it, if I tell you those three words, you'll stay?"

"If you say them *and* mean them," she underscored, "yes, I'll stay."

His eyes held hers for what felt like an eternity. And then he said, "I love you."

Morgan wasn't kidding when he'd said it wasn't easy for him to utter the words. The man seemed positively pained. "Now say it as if someone *wasn't* putting a match to your feet."

Gathering her closer so that her body fit against his, Morgan looked down into her face.

"I love you, Kelsey. God knows I don't want to, but there's nothing I can do about it. When I thought about never seeing you again, it made me feel so hollow inside, so empty, I could hardly stand it. I don't want to live like that. I don't want to feel empty, having each day that goes by exactly like the one before it and the one after it. I want life to be a surprise again, the way it was when we were together."

This wasn't any easier to say, but he knew it was the only way. And she deserved to know what he was feeling.

"I want to be part of something. I want to be part of you, part of your family. I want the whole nine yards." He framed her face, loving her so much that it hurt. "Because living the way I was before you changed everything wasn't living at all. It was just existing."

She stared at him, stunned. His voice echoed in her head and she was afraid that she imagined all this. "Are you saying what I think you're saying?"

"Only if you think I'm proposing. Because I am. Badly," he acknowledged, knowing his limitations. "But then, nobody has ever accused me of being a smooth talker."

"Oh, I don't know." The grin in her eyes filtered down to her lips. "Sounds pretty smooth to me."

Thank God she was going to stay. He wasn't too late. "Then are you saying yes?"

He saw her eyes crinkle, the smile there making her eyes sparkle. "I've been saying yes all along, you big idiot. You just weren't listening."

"I thought you originally told me that there were no strings attached."

Her slim shoulders moved up and then down. "I lied. I knew that if you suspected how I felt, you would have lost no time running for the hills. You almost did anyway."

Morgan grinned at her as he drew his hand through her hair. "The hills are highly overrated."

She'd made a run for them a time or two herself. "Tell me about it."

He shook his head. "Maybe later. Right now, we've got three weeks to catch up on and I intend to start right now." He began to unbutton her blouse slowly.

She felt the chills beginning. "I love a take-charge guy."

Morgan laughed then, really laughed. "The hell you do. You like bossing me around."

But it didn't matter. They had the rest of their lives to sort out their boundaries, he thought, and right now, all he wanted to do was merge those boundaries and lose himself in her.

It was the one place he felt at home.

Epilogue

Déjà vu.

This had *to be déjà vu,* Kelsey had thought.

Eight and a half months ago, Kelsey recalled, she'd gone through the very same thing: burst through the hospital doors practically before the electronic eye had time to pull them automatically back, her heart lodged in the middle of her throat.

Except that eight and a half months ago it had been fear that had been coursing through her veins. This time it had been anticipation and excitement that surged through her. And, eight and a half months ago, her mother had sworn her to secrecy, so she'd made her break-neck odyssey alone.

It was no secret now what had sent her mother off to

the hospital, once again huddled in the backseat of Morgan's car while a siren pealed a warning for other cars to pull over.

Moreover, Kelsey had thought gratefully, she definitely wasn't alone. Morgan was driving and her father was in the backseat with her mother, holding tightly on to her hand and telling her to hang on, that everything was going to be all right.

Not only was her father here with her, but her brothers and their wives, too, and Cody. They had all come, splitting up in two vehicles that had followed Morgan's, staying closer than shadows.

The only calm one in the bunch, relatively speaking, had been Cody. The little boy was more excited about the prospect that sometime during this special night, Santa would make an appearance and leave presents not only beneath his Christmas tree, but the one he'd just left behind at his grandparents' house. After all, it was Christmas Eve. The idea that a baby was about to make his or her appearance in the world any minute now came in as a very distant second.

Cody had wanted to ride to the hospital with "Uncle Morgan," hoping to be allowed to man the siren or the flashing lights. Trent had managed to convince the boy that it would be more fun on the return trip, when things weren't so hectic. Cody had reluctantly agreed, but only after Morgan had promised him that he could indeed turn on the siren for a minute.

Morgan.

Her Morgan.

As his wife of two months, she had the right to think of him that way. Funny how this baby had brought them initially together and now everything had come full circle.

Arriving at Blair Memorial, Morgan had pulled up in front of one of the hospital's valets. The latter, wearing a Santa cap, looked uncertainly at the flashing lights atop freshly promoted Detective Donnelly's car. His confusion grew as two more cars pulled up directly behind the first, and people started pouring out.

"Got a woman about to give birth," Morgan called out. Instantly, the second valet rushed off to fetch a wheelchair, the bells tied to his shoes jangling as he ran.

The smell of pine greeted them the moment Bryan pushed Kate's wheelchair into the E.R. waiting area. There was a Christmas tree next to the entrance. They were the only ones there. From all appearances, the hospital was experiencing a slow night.

That changed the moment her family came pouring in, Kelsey observed.

"She's going to be fine," Morgan had whispered in her ear as a nurse and an orderly took her mother and father to the maternity floor. Morgan pressed for the next available elevator car.

"Of course she is," Kelsey had retorted, her voice firm to convince herself.

That had been five hours ago.

Now, here they all were, crowded into the maternity floor waiting area. Cody was curled up in his mother's lap, asleep despite his efforts to remain awake. The rest of them were watching the doorway intently for any signs of someone coming to notify them that the newest Marlowe had finally arrived.

The air was thick with tension.

"Something's wrong," Kelsey said suddenly, unable to rein in her agitation.

"Some babies take longer than others," Miranda tried to reassure her.

Kelsey fisted her hands at her sides. "But her water broke," she insisted. Weren't babies supposed to come popping out right after that? Wasn't that why they'd raced to the hospital like that?

"Doesn't mean anything," Laurel told her, slowly stroking her son's hair as he went on sleeping. "It can still take a long time."

Kelsey wasn't convinced. "I'm going to find someone to ask," she declared, heading for the doorway.

But just as she was about to explode out into the festively decorated hallway, her father, dressed in green scrubs, cut her off at the threshold.

Bryan Marlowe grinned from ear to ear and looked almost like a teenager.

Instantly, everyone was on their feet except for Laurel. They circled him like hungry birds around a crust of bread.

"Well?" Kelsey demanded.

"It's a boy. Born one minute after midnight," her father announced proudly.

"I think there's something in the hospital guidelines that says you can't have twelve people at a bedside," the night nurse declared as she walked into Kate Marlowe's room and saw the crowd gathered around the maternity floor's only new patient in the last twelve hours.

"Oh, please," Kate entreated the older woman. "Just for a few minutes. It's Christmas," she added as a finalizing argument.

Bryan smiled warmly at his wife, looking down at the son who measured his age in hours. "Yes," he agreed. "It certainly is."

Morgan, his arm around Kelsey's waist, bent his head and kissed her hair softly. He'd never thought that he could feel this way again. That anything would cause his heart to open like this.

"This give you any ideas?" he asked Kelsey in a low whisper.

An expression he couldn't quite fathom was on her lips. "I was going to save this for later," Kelsey answered, "but I guess now's as good a time as any to tell you."

Puzzled, he stared at her. "Tell me what?"

Her face lit up as she whispered, "Merry Christmas, Morgan. You're going to be a daddy."

Speechless, overjoyed, Morgan swept his wife up into his arms and kissed her in full view of everyone—including his newest brother-in-law. It certainly was a Merry Christmas, he thought. From this day forward.

* * * * *

Don't miss Marie Ferrarella's next romance,
THE CAVANAUGH CODE,
available December 2009
from Silhouette Romantic Suspense!

Celebrate 60 years of pure reading
pleasure with Harlequin®!
Just in time for the holidays,
Silhouette Special Edition® is proud to present
New York Times *bestselling author*
Kathleen Eagle's
ONE COWBOY, ONE CHRISTMAS

Rodeo rider Zach Beaudry was a travelin' man—
until he broke down in middle-of-nowhere South
Dakota during a deep freeze. That's when an angel
came to his rescue....

"Don't die on me. Come on, Zel. You know how much I love you, girl. You're all I've got. Don't do this to me here. Not *now*."

But Zelda had quit on him, and Zach Beaudry had no one to blame but himself. He'd taken his sweet time hitting the road, and then miscalculated a shortcut. For all he knew he was a hundred miles from gas. But even if they were sitting next to a pump, the ten dollars he had in his pocket wouldn't get him out of South Dakota, which was not where he wanted to be right now. Not even his beloved pickup truck, Zelda, could get him much of anywhere on fumes. He was sitting out in the cold in the middle of nowhere. And getting colder.

He shifted the pickup into Neutral and pulled hard

on the steering wheel, using the downhill slope to get her off the blacktop and into the roadside grass, where she shuddered to a standstill. He stroked the padded dash. "You'll be safe here."

But Zach would not. It was getting dark, and it was already too damn cold for his cowboy ass. Zach's battered body was a barometer, and he was feeling South Dakota, big time. He'd have given his right arm to be climbing into a hotel hot tub instead of a brutal blast of north wind. The right was his free arm anyway. Damn thing had lost altitude, touched some part of the bull and caused him a scoreless ride last time out.

It wasn't scoring him a ride this night, either. A carload of teenagers whizzed by, topping off the insult by laying on the horn as they passed him. It was at least twenty minutes before another vehicle came along. He stepped out and waved both arms this time, damn near getting himself killed. Whatever happened to *do unto others?* In places like this, decent people didn't leave each other stranded in the cold.

His face was feeling stiff, and he figured he'd better start walking before his toes went numb. He struck out for a distant yard light, the only sign of human habitation in sight. He couldn't tell how distant, but he knew he'd be hurting by the time he got there, and he was counting on some kindly old man to be answering the door. No shame among the lame.

It wasn't like Zach was fresh off the operating table—it had been a few months since his last round of repairs—but he hadn't given himself enough time. He'd lopped a couple of weeks off the near end of the doc's estimated recovery time, rigged up a brace, done some heavy-duty taping and climbed onto another bull. Hung in there for five seconds—four seconds past feeling the pop in his hip and three seconds short of the buzzer.

He could still feel the pain shooting down his leg with every step. Only this time he had to pick the damn thing up, swing it forward and drop it down again on his own.

Pride be damned, he just hoped *somebody* would be answering the door at the end of the road. The light in the front window was a good sign.

The four steps to the covered porch might as well have been four hundred, and he was looking to climb them with a lead weight chained to his left leg. His eyes were just as screwed up as his hip. Big black spots danced around with tiny red flashers, and he couldn't tell what was real and what wasn't. He stumbled over some shrubbery, steadied himself on the porch railing and peered between vertical slats.

There in the front window stood a spruce tree with a silver star affixed to the top. Zach was pretty sure the red sparks were all in his head, but the white lights twinkling by the hundreds throughout the huge tree, those were real. He wasn't too sure about the woman hanging the shiny balls. Most of her hair was caught up on her head and fastened in a curly clump, but the light captured by the escaped bits crowned her with a golden halo. Her face was a soft shadow, her body a willowy silhouette beneath a long white gown. If this was where the mind ran off to when cold started shutting down the rest of the body, then Zach's final worldly thought was, *This ain't such a bad way to go.*

If she would just turn to the window, he could die looking into the eyes of a Christmas angel.

* * * * *

*Could this woman from Zach's past
get the lonesome cowboy to come in
from the cold...for good?
Look for
ONE COWBOY, ONE CHRISTMAS
by Kathleen Eagle
Available December 2009
from Silhouette Special Edition®*

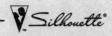

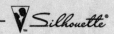
Silhouette®

SPECIAL EDITION

**FROM *NEW YORK TIMES* AND *USA TODAY*
BESTSELLING AUTHOR**

KATHLEEN EAGLE

ONE COWBOY,
One Christmas

When bull rider Zach Beaudry appeared
out of thin air on Ann Drexler's ranch,
she thought she was seeing a ghost of
Christmas past. And though Zach had
no memory of their night of passion years
ago, they were about to share a future
he would never forget.

*Available December 2009
wherever books are sold.*

SSE65493

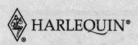

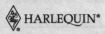

REQUEST YOUR FREE BOOKS!
2 FREE NOVELS PLUS 2 FREE GIFTS!

SPECIAL EDITION®
Life, Love and Family!

YES! Please send me 2 FREE Silhouette Special Edition® novels and my 2 FREE gifts (gifts are worth about $10). After receiving them, if I don't wish to receive any more books, I can return the shipping statement marked "cancel." If I don't cancel, I will receive 6 brand-new novels every month and be billed just $4.24 per book in the U.S. or $4.99 per book in Canada. That's a savings of at least 15% off the cover price! It's quite a bargain! Shipping and handling is just 50¢ per book.* I understand that accepting the 2 free books and gifts places me under no obligation to buy anything. I can always return a shipment and cancel at any time. Even if I never buy another book from Silhouette, the two free books and gifts are mine to keep forever.

235 SDN EYN4   335 SDN EYPG

Name	(PLEASE PRINT)	

Address		Apt. #

City	State/Prov.	Zip/Postal Code

Signature (if under 18, a parent or guardian must sign)

Mail to the **Silhouette Reader Service:**
IN U.S.A.: P.O. Box 1867, Buffalo, NY 14240-1867
IN CANADA: P.O. Box 609, Fort Erie, Ontario L2A 5X3

Not valid to current subscribers of Silhouette Special Edition books.

Want to try two free books from another line?
Call 1-800-873-8635 or visit www.morefreebooks.com.

* Terms and prices subject to change without notice. Prices do not include applicable taxes. Sales tax applicable in N.Y. Canadian residents will be charged applicable provincial taxes and GST. Offer not valid in Quebec. This offer is limited to one order per household. All orders subject to approval. Credit or debit balances in a customer's account(s) may be offset by any other outstanding balance owed by or to the customer. Please allow 4 to 6 weeks for delivery. Offer available while quantities last.

Your Privacy: Silhouette is committed to protecting your privacy. Our Privacy Policy is available online at www.eHarlequin.com or upon request from the Reader Service. From time to time we make our lists of customers available to reputable third parties who may have a product or service of interest to you. If you would prefer we not share your name and address, please check here. ☐

SSE09R

HARLEQUIN® HISTORICAL:
Where love is timeless

From chivalrous knights
to roguish rakes, look for the
variety Harlequin® Historical
has to offer every month.

www.eHarlequin.com

Silhouette®

COMING NEXT MONTH
Available November 24, 2009

#2011 ONE COWBOY, ONE CHRISTMAS—Kathleen Eagle
When bull rider Zach Beaudry appeared out of thin air on Ann Drexler's ranch, she thought she was seeing a ghost of Christmas past. And though Zach had no memory of their night of passion years ago, they were about to share a future he would never forget.

#2012 CHRISTMAS AT BRAVO RIDGE—Christine Rimmer
Bravo Family Ties
Lovers turned best friends Matt Bravo and Corrine Lonnigan had been there, done that with each other, and had a beautiful daughter. But their affair was ancient history…until old flames reignited over the holidays—and Corrine made Matt a proud daddy yet again!

#2013 A COLD CREEK HOLIDAY—RaeAnne Thayne
The Cowboys of Cold Creek
Christmas had always made designer Emery Kendall sad. But this Cold Creek Christmas was different—she rediscovered her roots… and found the gift of true love with rancher Nate Cavazos, whose matchmaking nieces steered Emery and Nate to the mistletoe.

#2014 A NANNY UNDER THE MISTLETOE—
Teresa Southwick
The Nanny Network
Libby Bradford had nothing in common with playboy Jess Donnelly—except for their love of the very special little girl in Jess and Libby's care. But the more time Libby spent with her billionaire boss, the more the mistletoe beckoned.…

#2015 A WEAVER HOLIDAY HOMECOMING—Allison Leigh
Men of the Double-C Ranch
Former agent Ryan Clay just wanted to forget his past. Then Dr. Mallory Keegan came to town—with the child he never knew he had. Soon, Ryan discovered the joy only a Christmas spent with the little girl—and her beautiful Aunt Mallory—could bring.

#2016 THE TEXAS TYCOON'S CHRISTMAS BABY—
Brenda Harlen
The Foleys and the McCords
When Penny McCord found out her lover Jason Foley was using her to get info about her family's jewelry-store empire, she was doubly devastated—for Penny was pregnant. Would a Christmas miracle reunite them…and reconcile their feuding families for good?

SSECNMBPA1109